HEARTS ARE JERKS

GABRIELLE HARBOWY

HEARTS ARE JERKS

GABRIELLE HARBOWY

HEART BOW BOOKS

ISBN paperback 978-1-7345526-0-7

Also by Gabrielle Harbowy

Complete Guide to Writing for Young Adults, Vol. 1
When the Hero Comes Home
When the Villain Comes Home
When the Hero Comes Home 2
Of the Essence
Pathfinder Tales: Gears of Faith

DEDICATION

To you
For following your heart
Even when it isn't easy.

CHAPTER 1

FIVE-THIRTY in the morning is an hour I've heard of but rarely seen. Mom's flight is at eight, so all of us are sprawled on her fluffy white bedspread in our pajamas to keep her company and help her with the last minute packing.

All of us is me, Dad, and Brenna, Dad's girlfriend.

And by helping, I mostly mean heckling.

"Did you pack Tina's birthday present?" Dad asks.

"Yes, Jeff." Mom rolls her eyes, but she still digs around in her carry-on to double check. Dad snickers, and Brenna chides him lightly with a shoulder-bump.

"Is there a card?" I ask. "I didn't get to sign the card."

Mom clears her throat. "So…"

Brenna takes over where Mom tapers off. "Allie, I think what your mom means is she's already written something mushy in it that we wouldn't want to see." Mom's furious blush is confirmation enough that Brenna is right.

"Ew, mushy grown-up stuff," I tease them, like I used to when I was a kid, and slide off the bed. "I'll get another card from my room."

I keep a box of blank greeting cards in my desk drawer. I buy them whenever I see one that's pretty or cool. I flip through them and stop at one with a big, crazy steampunk-looking cake on it. It's three tiers, all woodgrain and bronze. Some of the gears are bumpy with raised glitter accents, and there's a crank that looks like it could power the whole thing to life.

I think about writing something personal, but I'm barely conscious and even if I was awake, I'm not sure I'd know what to say. Mom gets to visit Tina pretty often, but Tina doesn't come here much. She doesn't totally click with the rest of us the way Brenna does. I like her and stuff, but she's always a little stiff and awkward when she's here, even though she and Mom and Dad all went to high school and college together. I don't even know if this card is her style, but nobody can hate a birthday card.

I keep the card sweet and simple, with plenty of room for Dad and Brenna to add messages, too. Just "Happy birthday! Love, Alicía."

My rummaging for an envelope rouses the big fluffy lump at the foot of my bed. Ozone stretches, yawns, and hops down to the floor.

I shuffle back to Mom's room with card and pen, and hand both to my dad. He signs and passes them to Brenna, who signs and puts the card in the envelope. "Maria," she says to get Mom's attention, and gives her the card. Mom has turned away from her open suitcase for maybe ten seconds, but that's more than enough time for the cat to make his move. We all watch, three of us tittering, Mom with her hands on her hips, while the cat makes himself comfortable in a lazy sprawl across her clothes like he's been there the whole time.

"It begins." With a sigh, Mom lifts the purring monster

and dumps him on me. He's all floof, warm and smug. A nest of long, pale orange-white hairs remains behind him. The cat sheds on *everything*. We call his fur-drifts the Ozone layer. "Here. You get cat duty."

"He's helping!"

"Yes. He's just as helpful as the rest of you." Mom smiles when she says it, though, and I know she's going to miss us. The cat tries one more feint toward the suitcase, but I've got a solid grip on him. He gives up, squirms in my arms to get comfortable, and then goes limp.

After the bag is zipped, I let Ozone down to the bed and give Mom a hug. "Have fun, and don't worry about us. I promise I won't take candy from strangers, I won't steal library books, and I won't go joyriding in your car. Oh, and Dad and Brenna promise, too."

"I'm not signing my name to the candy thing," Dad says, which makes Mom laugh. He gets up and gives her a hug. "Go have fun, and say hi for us."

While Tina is someone Mom visits, Brenna is family. She talks to me like I'm a real person with thoughts and opinions about things outside myself, and critical thinking skills. My parents sometimes treat me like a little kid. Brenna says they don't mean to, it's just that they're trying to hold on to when I was small and all theirs, instead of having to think about how close I am to leaving home and going out into a world they can't protect me from. I don't know why *they* don't just tell me that. Brenna rolls her eyes and says it's because they're parents. She's careful not to say that in front of them.

I used to think "parent" and "grown-up" were the same thing. Now I know there's a big difference that has nothing to do with whether a person's had kids. Brenna isn't a parent, but she's sometimes more a parent to me than my parents are, because I can go to her and I know she'll be honest with me instead of trying to water things down or save me from the world. And probably because she's a therapist, so she's trained to understand people. I'm sixteen. I'm going off on my own soon. She knows I need to be introduced to the world, not shielded from it.

Brenna is Dad's girlfriend and Tina is Mom's girlfriend. That's something they've never tried to hide from me. And yes, Mom and Dad are totally still together, too. It's not like they're separated but still living in the same house, or anything like that. Technically, what they have is called polyamory. It's an "alternative relationship," but it doesn't feel alternative to me. It feels comfortable and, honestly, pretty cool. I look at all the books and movies and things where there's someone cheating on someone else, or there's a love triangle and everybody's jealous, and it all just seems so stupid. I mean, if they were just open about it, everyone could be happy. Right?

Then again, without the lying and the sneaking and the worrying about getting caught, or the angst about which boy to choose, there'd be no conflict. Brenna says people like the drama because they crave the resolution. Take away the drama and there's no story. I don't know… I'm pretty sure freaking out about who people are sleeping with isn't the only story in the world. Why have a fit over who someone else loves? But people like to obsess over other people's bedroom business, I guess.

My black nightshirt is now pale angora from the cat. When I take it off, fur goes everywhere and clings to my face, making it feel like I've just walked through cobwebs. I'd wanted to go back to bed and skip my shower, but now I feel gross. Besides, maybe a shower will help me wake up.

When I shuffle downstairs, washed and dressed, Brenna is already on the couch looking ready for the day, hair in a neat brown ponytail, holding her smartphone in one hand and a big mug of coffee in the other. Brenna's therapy office is in the basement, with a separate entrance for her clients. She has a nice short commute.

"Hey," Brenna says. "Quick thinking with the card. There's coffee in the pot."

"Thanks." Coffee is a gross but necessary evil, especially on sleepy mornings like this one. The only way I can drink it is when it's mostly warm milk and sugar—*cafe con leche*, we call it, even though mine is more *leche* than *cafe*—but the heat and caffeine make it worthwhile. I just wish it would taste the way it smells.

The milk cools the coffee enough for me to drink most of it in one go, on the way to the door. Then I stop. "Mug goes back in the kitchen," I tell myself. It's not unusual for me to quasi-sleepwalk my way to school, but it's embarrassing when it's obvious.

"And shoes. You might want shoes," Brenna calls after me.

I look down at my feet. I swear the blue seams on my socks are curved into two smug grins. She might be right. The ankle-height brown boots I wore yesterday are still by the door. They'll be good if it rains. I slip them on and crouch to tie the laces.

"Is Miss K coming over tonight?" she asks me.

"Yeah, but we might go shopping first."

"Okay," Brenna says. "I won't expect you before… six?" She says it like a question; by nodding I'm committing myself to six o'clock.

Shoes. Backpack. Keys. Phone. Umbrella. No mug. School.

CHAPTER 2

BECAUSE I remember my umbrella, of course it's not raining. The air is still damp with dew, but with the way the sunlight sparkles across it, it looks like it might be the first really nice spring-like day we've had so far. I'm tempted to cut through the little park on the way to school, but one squishy step off the sidewalk tells me that the ground is still more damp than not. My neighbor across the street, Loudon, is also walking down the block. Sometimes when the weather's bad enough for her mom to give her a ride, she offers me a ride, too. I wave to be polite and she lifts a hand back, but we don't cross the street to walk together or anything. We're not that close, and anyway, she's got the tell-tale hot pink cords of headphones emerging from her hair. After school, I'll have Keisha to make the return walk with me.

Keisha comes home with me after school on Fridays and sleeps over. It's a thing we've been doing since before we were officially together-together. Mom and Dad and Brenna all love her, and they know we're girlfriends. Keisha is sure her parents would *not* be fine with it, so we keep things under the radar around them and when we're out anywhere. Commander B. Tyrone Harris is a career Navy officer and super traditional. He works at the Pentagon, in the kind of job where you can't ask him what happened at the office today, because he can't tell you. LaShaun Harris, Keisha's mom, is an office manager at the Museum of African American Art. I'd never say so to Keisha, but I think if their daughter was dating a black girl, they'd have an easier time with the "girl" part.

When I met Keisha, I was volunteering in the library at lunch, and she was reading Shakespeare. The complete Shakespeare. For fun. I asked her which play was her favorite, and she said, "I don't know yet. You can't have a favorite until you've read them all." It turned out she was in Drama Club and serious about acting. Reading Shakespeare was a way to search for monologues she could use for acting competitions, instead of just preparing the same passages everybody else always uses. But still.

I was in ninth grade and I considered myself a bookworm, but I'd never met anyone whose idea of fun was reading Shakespeare cover to cover. That takes bookworm to a whole new level. I admit, there might have been swooning.

I was obsessed with her in a way that wasn't just friendship, but that I didn't know how to express. Her skin is smooth, airbrush-smooth, like deep brown satin. Even though her brain is amazing too, and we can talk about anything and giggle for hours, I could never stop thinking about touching her. It was making me really weird around her. Then one night when she was staying over, she told me she was bi. I scooted over and gave her a big hug. Even though I'd meant it to be supportive, like a "thank you for trusting me with something so personal" thing, what came out of my mouth was "me, too." I was worried she'd be mad—I'd taken her moment and made it about me—but she was actually relieved. Hugging turned into kissing turned into a really late night of figuring stuff out, and we've been dating ever since. Just thinking about that night, even now, makes me tingle a little.

A school bus is letting out just as I get to the doors, so I let the tide of people carry me inside. I shuffle down the main hall and divert at the double doors to the library. I volunteer in the school library most days during lunch—and before classes too, on days when I'm not a shambling sleep-monster. Which means that on days like today when I *am* a shambling sleep-monster, I can use the faculty vending machine in the staff hallway behind the library. The price on it has been set to just a quarter, and half the time if you hit the coin return just right, you can get the quarter back.

Volunteering in the library has already gotten me a paying part-time job at the public library after school. The part of me that doesn't still want to be an astronaut or a rock star has decided to go into information sciences when I grow up. I kind of love the Dewey Decimal system.

I hover my finger over the diet button. The caffeine is what I really need, but I could use the sugar boost, too. But I don't want to be hyper in class. I look up at the clock: five minutes until first bell. I make a quick decision and push the button for the full jet-fuel experience. I've got about two minutes to gulp it down. I promise myself I'll atone by having the salad bar at lunch.

Halfway through second period, I realize I forgot to try the trick with the coin return. Chugging the sugar and caffeine helped, though, and somehow I stay awake until lunch.

Our cafeteria is arranged with café-style seating, with tables for two or four. Keisha and I almost always sit together, and this semester Andrew's been joining us, too. Kids move tables around all the time, just like restaurants do, so often we'll end up with six. There's an unspoken rule that two people at a two-person table want their privacy, but sitting at a bigger table invites company.

I get in line for salad, and by the time I'm done loading a plate with vegetables and cold chicken strips, Keisha is already at our usual table. It's teriyaki day in the regular line, so I think I chose wisely.

When I sit down next to Keisha, we squeeze hands under the table. It's what we do when we're someplace where we can't kiss hello or good bye. She's got her hair straightened today, and she's wearing a men's style button down shirt, pink, unbuttoned at the collar just far enough to show a string of garnet beads and a peek of gray tank top underneath.

"So dapper," I say, and she grins.

"It looked better with the skirt, but if I'm trying on shoes…" She makes a face, either at the idea of giving some stranger an accidental peek—or just at the idea of matching a skirt with running shoes. I think both would bother her equally.

"Dressy shirts with jeans are hot," I answer.

"What's hot?" Andrew, as if summoned by the chance to steer a conversation toward the gutter, sets his tray down opposite mine.

Keisha tries three times to spear a piece of chicken on her flimsy plastic fork before switching tactics and scooping it up instead. "Tonight. I need gym shoes. So sexy."

Andrew smirks at both of us. "Ooh, lace-up action. Do you need a ride?"

It's super generous of him to offer, but this is Andrew. The spark in his eyes, all animated and full of potential, means he's setting up for whatever he's going to say next.

I play along. "What'll it cost us?"

He pretends to mull it over. "You both try on lingerie and take pictures?"

I laugh, trying to ignore the tingle that runs through me and the way the back of my neck suddenly feels sweaty.

Keisha leans across the table and looks him right in the eyes. "You're on," she says, then sits back and sneaks me a sidelong wink.

Andrew seems as stunned as I am. He recovers his poise quickly, but there's a moment where his jaw actually goes slack. He lifts a long-fingered hand to flick hair out of his face. He's pale and blond, with that kind of coloring that always wants an excuse to turn red, either through flushing from exertion or burning from the slightest exposure to the sun. The gesture isn't about his hair—I suspect he's trying to hide his sudden blush. I kind of love that he blushes.

"Allie?" He turns to me. "As the party of the third part, you get an opportunity to veto." Andrew wants to go to law school, and definitely has the manner for it, when he's not thinking with his crotch.

I don't need time to consider it. I'm enjoying this too much. "Wouldn't veto for the world."

"O-okay." He exhales quickly, straightening as he breathes in. "It's a date. I mean, technically it's *your* date, but… okay. Meet me at my car after late bell?"

The whole rest of the day, I'm stuck on a loop imagining what putting on a show for Andrew would be like, but I know he's not going to expect us to actually do it. If he was the kind of guy who insisted we owed it to him or something, I wouldn't be dating him.

Oh, right. This is where I mention that I'm dating Andrew, too.

Andrew waits for us by his mom's hand-me-down Prius, his car the same pale cornflower blue as his eyes. The trunk is already open, with his beaten-up cello case moved aside to make room for our backpacks. Ki gives him a hug and a peck on the cheek. When she's done and climbing into the back seat, I give him a warm kiss. It's only about a fifteen-minute walk to the Metro station, but it's getting toward rush hour so the trains are all full. Even more annoying is the walk home afterwards—with packages, in the dark and possibly in the rain. Having a ride is a huge convenience.

Andrew is a year older than us. He got exposed to chickenpox really bad, right when he was supposed to start kindergarten, and they kept him back a whole year. He couldn't start school until the next fall. That sounds kind of extreme to me. I mean, it's *kindergarten*. It's not like you stay contagious as a carrier forever, or like missing a month of playing with blocks is impossible to make up. You can practice the ABC song at home. But, whatever. Fast forward to now and it means that he has a real license, not just a learner's permit like the rest of us.

My dad keeps saying he'll take me out to practice driving sometime soon, in a safe place like a parking lot, or maybe the bumper car ride at the fair. Driving is a grown up thing, so I don't think I can hop up and down and ask if it's time yet now, like a kid would. Still, I'm pretty excited. I like to sit in the front passenger seat and watch people drive, and I've read up on driving, too. In Dewey Decimal terms, transportation is in the social sciences, which is the 300s, but driving is in technology, about 629 or so. I think it's interesting that cars and the use of cars are in different places. Anyway, I've passed my written test and done everything except get behind the wheel. By this time next year, maybe I'll be the one to drive us to the mall.

The lingerie store is our first stop, so that we can meet our end of the bargain. Keisha is brave and outgoing and pleasantly devious in ways I don't think I could ever be, so I'm usually happy enough to follow her lead. If I don't want to, I can always say so, but her ideas are usually fun. Like taking Andrew up on his offer. I'm a little nervous, but I know she's got a plan and I'm too curious to stop her now.

We each pick a couple of things to try on. I choose a satiny nightgown in forest green, with a matching cover-up robe, and a black lace leotard. I have my period and that gives me a moment's pause, but you have to keep your underwear on while you're trying lingerie on, anyway. Keisha picks a camisole and silky shorts, black lace accents over pink. Then we slip into a changing room together.

"Things seem good with your boy," she observes while we undress. "Almost six months?"

"Just about," I agree. "Things are good. I think this is him trying to be inclusive and stuff."

She smirks. "So, in addition to thinking two girls together are hot, he's *also* cool with the idea of you dating more than one person."

"Exactly." I pull the robe off the hanger. Keisha takes my phone out of my discarded jeans, unlocks it by holding it up to scan my face, and fiddles with settings. "What are you up to?" I ask her.

"Just turning off your auto-focus." She turns the phone around to show me a snapshot of a green blur. I laugh. It's perfect.

"Your parents are good role models," she adds. She keeps the phone moving while she clicks shots of the clothes still on their hangers.

"Yeah. He hasn't really talked about it with them, but you know, he sees how casual they are. It's not like my mom's just pretending to be cool with Brenna, or something."

Keisha hands me the phone and tugs the silk camisole into place. When she strikes a pose, I get right up close to her elbow so that it fills the frame. Click. Send.

"Have you... you know... ?"

"Have I... ?" I prompt. She gives me a Look with a capital-L. "No! God, no. Nothing past kissing." My cheeks burn, and I suddenly feel very naked. I throw my shirt at her face. She catches it and throws it back. She's hinted at the question a few times, but this is the first time she's come out and asked me if I've gone all the way with him yet.

"What, are boys suddenly gross or something?" she teases.

"No, I just—" I clear my throat, take a breath, and start again with my voice lower. If they think we're playing around in here, they'll throw us out. Plus you never know if some girl from school is just on the other side of the partition, recording your antics on her phone. "I wouldn't mind if he turned up the heat, but you push all my buttons just fine. So... no rush, you know?"

I guess it's natural to wonder how it would be different with a boy, but it's a lot more complicated with a boy, too. There's pregnancy obviously; that's the big one. But also, protection is evidence that can be found by parents, and that leads to lectures and stupid advice you already know, and maybe getting grounded. If girls at school find out, to your face they're all interested and they ask questions about what it's like, but then they call you a slut behind your back. If boys find out, they high-five your boyfriend while they glare at you like they're upset the candy store is only open for someone else.

That stuff hasn't happened to me, obviously, but I've seen it happen enough. This girl Faith lost her virginity over winter vacation and told one person, and it was all over the school by lunch. Kids are jerks.

Keisha clears her throat. "So..."

"Hmm?" She's hesitant in a way that's not like her, fiddling with the spaghetti straps on my shoulders. She's not usually hesitant about anything. I know her tone, though. It's the same tone that was in my voice when I told her about Andrew. "What's his name?" I ask.

She looks at me wide-eyed, like I must be psychic. I'm happy to let her keep thinking it. It keeps her on her toes.

"Sean. He's in my martial arts class at the Y. He goes to Central, too."

Central High is an absurdly big school, bigger than some liberal arts colleges. It's totally possible to have people in your graduating class that you've never met. So even though he goes to our school, a first name without context doesn't mean much to me.

"Do you just like him, or are you guys going out, or… ?"

"We've had a few dates," she admits. "I didn't want to say anything beforehand in case it turned out to be nothing, but now it looks like it might not be nothing. Are you mad? I told him I had a girlfriend and he was cool with it."

Usually, I hate being asked if I'm mad. Not when I can tell she's asking for reassurance, though. No wonder she was suddenly extra curious about my dates with a boy. "Not mad, excited! When do we get to meet him?"

"Soon." She's blushing, and it's so adorable I just have to kiss her. Even if we do end up getting in trouble.

When we come out of the store, Andrew looks up from his phone and fans himself, like he's recovering from our texted peep show. He tries to peek in the bag to see what Keisha bought, but she doesn't let him get past the shielding bloom of red tissue paper that obscures the delights below. He says she's mean and turns to me for sympathy, but I just laugh at him. I get all warm and tingly watching them joke and punch each other on the arm, and then hug. They get along well, and it makes me happy. There's nothing more exciting than opaque tights in her shopping bag, but he doesn't need to know that.

One of the benefits of my parents' relationship is that I've got the master bedroom. They each have their own space, and they can share beds with each other or sleep alone as they choose to (which is most of the time, because my dad snores like whoa), but when we moved in together, they all agreed that they didn't want any one of them to be—or appear to be—at the top of a hierarchy. It's not the guy with his two sister-wives or anything like that, so Dad didn't want the big bedroom. So they all agreed they would give it to me. It's not that much bigger than the other bedrooms, but it has its own bathroom. That's the big bonus for me, and also it means more privacy for everyone. The other three bedrooms share the two hall bathrooms between them.

I put on some superhero movie that we can ignore as background noise, and we pile into my bed, sprawling and cuddling and treating each other like pillows that are just there for our convenience. Keisha has really sensitive earlobes, so I take one and nibble at it. That makes her whimper and squirm and want revenge. Today, revenge looks like pinning my wrists over my head while she straddles me, grinding her thigh between mine. "Payday?" she asks, and I nod. That's our code for my period, since I get it reliably at the end of the month, kind of exactly when I get paid.

Keisha, who has made me climax uncountable times, with clothes and without, nods but isn't deterred. I want to get out of my jeans and get my lips on her skin, but the way she rubs her strong thigh against me feels so good I can't bring myself to do anything but press myself up to her and enjoy it. My orgasm feels like a tingling that builds behind my pubic bone and gets stronger and stronger until I almost can't handle any more, and then it breaks and washes over me and my inner muscles start to pulse involuntarily, thumping like a fierce heartbeat inside me. When that happens, I cry out and reach for her, and finally she stretches out on top of me in a full-body hug while the tingles start to ease and fade.

We've just collapsed into a cozy heap again when I hear the rumble of the garage door. By the time Brenna comes up to say hi and make sure nothing is going on, we're cuddling innocently, watching a movie. She spots the shopping bag from the shoe store and asks what I got, so Keisha announces that she's apparently graduated to a size 8, and laments that her feet are never going to stop.

"I guess you guys really can't share shoes anymore," Brenna says.

"Cinderella's stepsister cut her toes off to fit into the glass slipper," I say. I'm helpful that way, especially when I'm in the cuddly post-climax glow.

"Cinderella's stepsister didn't have to run the mile twice a week in gym," Keisha answers, nudging me with her shoulder.

"Your dad will be home with dinner in an hour." Brenna blows us a kiss before wandering off.

I look Sean up on the school's intranet, with Ki hovering over my shoulder and guiding me. His last name is Wilson, and he's hot. The black and white photos from the school paper don't do him justice, but last year's yearbook has him in a loincloth thingy in a presentation for history class. And he's smart. Honor Society. Not bad. "Cute boy you got there. Double date?"

"Thought you'd never ask. What are you guys doing tomorrow?"

I reach for my phone. "Let's find out!"

Saturday is my date night with Andrew, but when we message him about it he's also into the double date idea. There's a lot of texting back and forth. Sean suggests a drive-in theater he knows. He used to work there during the summers and he can get us in for free. "Sounds fun," I say.

A movie is a safe date. It counts as hanging out, but if you don't like someone you don't have to talk to them. Then again, if Keisha likes him, he's probably good people. She's glad I think so, and she's got an extra bounce in her already energetic step when we head downstairs for dinner. Seeing her so happy soothes some of the butterflies in my stomach.

I didn't know drive-ins were still a thing, but sure enough, about half an hour into the heart of the suburbs there's a gravel lot with three big blank billboard screens set at skewed angles.

Sean is darker-skinned than Ki, but otherwise they could be siblings. They're both lazily muscular without looking like bodybuilders, both on the short side of average, but he still has a good few inches on her. They're cute together. I've never dated anyone of my own race and it's never been a big deal, but seeing them together makes me wonder what it would be like to date a Latino boy. It's not like we'd get fewer strange looks, because I don't get any now. Would there be any shared heritage or references that other people wouldn't get? Would it feel any more special or any closer?

Andrew and I are in the front and Ki and Sean are in the back. We stop at the gate and Sean works his magic, lowering his window and being charming with the ticket guy. I think there's a fist bump. We get waved on in without having to pay. Once we've found a good spot, Keisha and Sean get out and crunch across the gravel to the popcorn stand.

I may not have realized this was here, but apparently it's not a secret. The place is half full when we get there, and when I look around a little while later, it's packed.

"In our parents' day, this is probably where you had to come to make out," I say.

"And you probably had to hope nobody was peeking from car to car, looking for gossip they could spread."

"They only had their own word on it, though. No camera phones. No evidence."

"I don't think gossip needs evidence. The potential that it might be true is enough to fire people up, isn't it?"

I hadn't thought of it that way, but I guess so.

"So," Andrew continues, stealing a glance around before returning those blue eyes to me. "Wanna make out?"

"Quick," I answer, "before my girlfriend gets back." He laughs and kisses me. His lips are so different than Keisha's, but they still press perfectly against mine. Soon I'm only aware of his closeness and not of the passage of time, but he stops just as I start to melt into him and wish we had the privacy to do more. I whimper, and he grins at me.

Gravel crunches and scuffs, and my girlfriend is back with her boyfriend. And popcorn and drinks for four.

We snark during the movie, making fun of all the questionable costuming choices and the characters' bad decisions. It's nice, getting to see it on a big screen while knowing we're not pissing off the people around us with our commentary.

"So, your parents are cool with this?" Sean asks me as the credits roll.

"Her parents *are* this," Keisha answers.

"I live with my mom, my dad, and my dad's girlfriend, and they've been together all my life. Everybody's cool about it," I say, on cue.

Sean laughs. "Lucky guy."

"Ew," Keisha says, elbowing him. "That's her *dad*. Anyway, it's not like constant orgy. I think in all the times I've slept over, all I've ever overheard is your dad snoring."

"Lost opportunity, is all I'm saying," he answers.

"Ew, parents?" I remind him.

"Okay, okay. So, is it really all rosy? Isn't it ever… ?" He waves his hand. "You know… bitchy?"

"You mean are they jealous? Not that I've ever seen. It's pretty comfortable. Seriously."

He looks unconvinced, but it's not like I know some magic words to say to convince him.

Andrew drives us to the park, where we get out to stretch and walk around, which is nice after the confinement of the car. Technically the park closes at sundown, but as long as you're not doing anything suspicious, no one really cares. We pass a few people jogging with their dogs, coming the other way.

Sean and Keisha hold hands a lot, but she doesn't treat me like "just friends" to do it. He's conscious of making sure he respects the fact that there's more between us than that. Except for what feels like an "I have to see it to believe it" attitude toward my parents' situation, he seems to be keeping up with the rest of us well enough.

When we eventually perch on an empty picnic table, Sean

maneuvers Keisha next to me and sits at her other side. At some point he moves up onto the table behind her and starts rubbing her back. She's sitting between his legs, so one of his thighs is along my side. I don't even notice when my arm starts resting on his leg so I can hold hands with her, but he doesn't mind and I feel weirdly comfortable. At one point Andrew gives my butt a stealthy squeeze, and that makes me imagine all sorts of possibilities, even though I hadn't been thinking naughty thoughts before.

Andrew is always turned on. Usually he channels it into innuendo and harmless quips that let it dissipate out of his system, but sometimes he knows I'm kinda turned on, too.

After the movie, Andrew drives Ki and Sean to the Metro station, to go off on the rest of their date. Suddenly I have a weird sense of how my parents must feel when I go out, so before I've even really thought about it I'm asking if she has a sweater and giving them both all sorts of deliberately jumbled up parent-like advice. "Look both ways before washing your hands"—absurd stuff like that. But Ki can tell it comes from approval, so she's all glowy and giggly by the time they actually leave.

Andrew rests his arm around my shoulders. "Our little girl, all grown up."

I laugh and poke him in the ribs, right where I know he's ticklish.

We've got a reading assignment to do, but it's a book that's available on audio, so that's how Andrew and I are reading it. It might seem like a boring date, but I really like curling up on him, closing my eyes, and getting immersed in words and stories together. Afterwards, we can talk about it like we were both really there having the same experience with the characters, and that helps me remember it later.

For the test, of course, but beyond the test, too. My parents like that we actually study when we say we're going upstairs to study. We kill pixelated aliens together, too, but not until homework is done.

Tonight we go up to my room and listen to three chapters. Through the whole last chapter I pretend not to notice that his hand is on my ribs, alllllmost touching my breast. It feels nice. Warm. My door is open the requisite four inches, and at one point I hear Dad's footsteps walk by, stop, and move on, but he doesn't interrupt us or clear his throat or tell Andrew to move his hand. His footsteps just start again and fade off down the hall. Once Dad's made the rounds, I nudge Andrew's palm all the way onto my breast. He gives it a slow, healthy squeeze, then eases off to rest his fingers on my ribs again. I'm disappointed, but I respect it. I know he likes me, and he's attracted to me, or he wouldn't be here. I make it sting less by telling myself that he just has massive self-control.

After I shut the recording off, we sit in silence for a minute or so, pulling our thoughts together and slowly returning to the real world. Instead of commenting on Scout Finch, Andrew says, "What did you think of Sean?"

It takes me a minute to realize he's talking about Keisha's date, not some character I didn't remember from the book. I twist around in his arms just enough to look at him. It's hard to tell when he's serious, and I'm also looking for a hint of the motive behind the question. It sounds light and casual, but that doesn't mean it is. It could just be how he's playing it off.

"He's okay," I say. "What did you think?"

Andrew shrugs, pulling his laptop out of his backpack. "I don't know. He's okay. It's too early to tell." He pauses, studying me. "Still want to kill some aliens?"

I want to make out and feel his hands all over me, but I rally myself. "Of course. The universe isn't going to save itself."

CHAPTER 3

MONDAY on the way to lunch, Keisha tells me that Sean and Andrew have exchanged contact info through her, and they're planning to hang out after school at Andrew's and play video games. "Sean wants your number, too. Is that okay? I told him I wouldn't give it to him without asking you."

"Sure, that's fine." I can't imagine hanging out with him solo, just me and him, but I can see us all texting notes to each other or needing to make plans, or something. "If it's okay with you. I mean, I get it if you want to keep him to yourself."

That halts her in her steps, and I panic for a second because maybe she's taken it in some weird way that I didn't mean her to. But then she nudges shoulders with me and starts onward again. "I hadn't thought of it like that. That's sweet of you. But, no. It's cool. I like that you guys like him, too." We join the back of the cafeteria line. "Are you working after school? Maybe I'll come by the library for a while."

"After rehearsal? That would be great."

You'd never know what was on the menu by the smell in the cafeteria, except on pasta day. The garlic wafts over us in a wave at the door and Ki and I both look around suspiciously. "No vampires?" she asks me.

"I don't see any." That is, no one's just keeled over—or bolted away—from the stench. I like garlic, but the smell can be too much even for me. Yet, somehow, they still manage to make it taste completely bland.

We eat with Andrew, and Sean and a couple other people join us at our customary table. Brian DiFrancisco, my eternal lab partner due to our adjacent last names, joins us on days when his usual lunch companions are talking baseball. I don't think I've ever seen him on pasta day: he pulls all the whole garlic cloves out of his pasta sauce, lines them up on the side of his tray, and then smushes them into his bread like a topping. He does it with the careless nonchalance that marks it as a long-standing habit, and I think I'd remember if I'd seen him do that before. It looks… kind of interesting, actually, so I try it too. It works. There's a burst of flavor so strong it stings a little. He watches me, then smirks when I take another bite.

Keisha, who has opted for chicken cutlet without the garlic-heavy sauce, taps my leg under the table and hands me a plastic-wrapped mint. I laugh out loud. "Hint taken," I murmur, and she winks.

Sunday through Wednesday, I work at the public library after school, afternoon through closing. Sunday afternoon there's story time for the little kids, and story time is my favorite. Even when I'm not the one reading, I love the spell that books cast over all the kids. For entire minutes, some of them forget to fidget, or dig for treasure in their own noses, or beg their parents to take them somewhere with more toys. I love the stories, too. Kids' books are even cuter than kids. They have story time during the week, too, but it's while I'm in school. Over the summer, I'll get to be there for that.

There aren't many kids from my school who study or read at the library, since we can do most of that stuff online, and most of us have the internet at home. When I'm doing pick-up—collecting all the books people leave on the tables when they're done with them—I love when Keisha comes out to study. She always makes really weird improbable little stacks of books that have nothing to do with each other, or that suggest a messed up story. Sometimes it's the subjects, sometimes it's the titles, but I love that she leaves little presents all over the library to keep me entertained while I work. Today she leaves a book on fairies, with a book on archery, plus how to cook over a campfire. It's good for the library, too. The more books are left out, the more we have to check in—all books that are left out have to be checked back in before we shelve them. That might seem like a pain, but the more books we check back in, the busier our branch looks. I love that Keisha goes out of her way to make it fun for me.

Mom comes back from her trip looking relaxed and refreshed. Her hair is cut a little short, just above her shoulders, thick and wavy. It was halfway down her back when she left.

"I love it!" I tell her first thing, while we hug. "Too cute!" Her nails are painted copper like autumn leaves and her brows are thin. It looks like she and Tina went for the full spa treatment. I'm glad. Mom doesn't take many opportunities to focus on herself.

The next Friday is date night again, just me and Keisha, and everything's back to normal. No Andrew, no Sean, just us staying up late talking and messing around in bed and barely remembering to put some clothing on before we fall asleep.

Saturday afternoon, Dad drives Keisha home. Her mom meets us when we pull up into the guest spot in front of her apartment building. She wears her hair in braids coiled on top of her head, making her look a lot taller than she is. I think she's actually shorter than me, but you'd never know it from looking at her. It's not just her hair, either. She's got a commanding presence, like she's the queen of every room she walks into. I've honestly never noticed if I have to look downward at all to meet her eyes, because meeting her eyes kind of scares me a little.

"Well-behaved?" she asks my dad, as Keisha squeezes my shoulder and gets out of the car.

"As always," Dad says. From the front passenger seat I wave hello, and Ki's mom waves back. By then Keisha has come around the car to her mom, and they're already talking about plans for the rest of the day and turning to walk back inside by the time we pull away.

We're back out on the road when Dad says, "Does Keisha's mom know you two are..." He pauses, choosing his word, and I'm surprised how anxious I am about how he's going to finish the sentence. My stomach flutters a little. "... Cozy?"

It's not the word I was expecting, but I kind of like it. It sums everything up in such a tender way that I know my cheeks are burning crimson. "Noooo. Her parents would freak out."

Dad shrugs, the kind of shrug that usually means "I know you're wrong, but I'll let you figure it out on your own." Dad has some kind of computer security job with the government, but he doesn't talk about what agency he works for or what he does there. As a result, he's good at wordless commentary. He can answer without saying a thing, or make you feel like you've gotten an answer when you haven't. This shrug is the former. He's not going on record, but his opinion is clear.

"Okay, so maybe she wouldn't," I say, "but Keisha thinks she would, and it's got to be her choice, right?"

He inclines his head to that, conceding one point to me. "Fair enough. How do *you* feel about keeping it hidden?"

"It's fine." It's my standard answer and I say it without thinking. But is it? In the deliberate pause he leaves me before he responds, a lot of feelings well up and I push them back down. It's something I do a lot, but I never realized how automatic it is until just now.

"It's convenient, being able to hide it," I add. "We can sneak under the radar because people see what they want to see. If we were open, they'd still see what they wanted to see, but they'd interpret all the same things so differently… and that might take everything away. I mean, yeah, it's hard to watch what I say and do, and I'm always afraid I'll screw up and get her in trouble. It's nice to be able to hang out at home, where you guys are cool with things."

He chuckles under his breath. It's not a mean sound, but it makes me defensive anyway.

"What?"

"Oh," he says, shaking his head. "It's just, if you told me-at-your-age that I'd end up being one of the cool parents, I don't know if I would have believed you."

"Abi and Belo weren't cool parents?" It's what I've called my grandparents since as far back as I can remember; I've never called them *abuela* and *abuelo*. I don't know if they chose the nicknames or if I came up with them, but they stuck.

"They were strict and very Catholic. You see them now, in their mellow years, when their only job is to spoil you, not raise you. They threatened to disown me when I changed my name."

I'd never thought about what it would have been like for Dad growing up, especially in a much more conservative time. I knew they had named my dad Jesus, and that when he was eighteen he went to court and legally got it changed to Jeff. I'd always just thought it was a normal thing for someone to do. My dad was the first generation in his family to be born in this country, and maybe he wanted an American-sounding name. All through history classes, I've read about people who changed their names when they got here, or when they went into show business, so it doesn't seem weird to me. And I know lots of people who aren't religious, so I never really thought about how Dad hasn't raised me with any kind of religious background. I never thought about how it might have been a big fight.

"Oh. Because of Latino heritage, or because of religion?"

"There wasn't much difference between the two, when I was growing up. Anyway, here we are."

He stops the car and shifts it into park. I haven't been paying attention, just keeping one small corner of my brain alert to recognize when we pull into the driveway, but he hasn't taken us home.

We're in a cemetery. Green rolling hills dotted with headstones, with a single paved road winding between the different sections.

"Dad? Did someone die?" After the conversation we just had, I wonder if this is where Dad's parents will eventually be, but for now they're both very much alive. We only saw them last month.

He opens his door and gestures for me to get out, too. "You've been asking me for driving lessons since you got your permit. So, come and take it for a spin. It's the safest place in the world to drive, right? If you mess up big, you're already here."

Dad tosses his keys to me in a perfect arc over the top of the car. I reach out to pluck them out of the air… and miss. They jingle twice. Once when they bounce off my knuckles and again when they hit the ground. He laughs while I pick them up and I smile back, even though my mind is racing and I'm sure my cheeks are burning. Surprise driving lesson! I want to be excited about it, but it's too sudden and my brain feels too full.

Mostly, I just feel the crushing weight of wanting to impress him, and a sinking feeling because I'm obviously off to a great start.

Opening the door operates on the same theories and rules of physics on both sides of the car. It's pathetic that I have to tell myself this, but for a moment I've totally blanked on the fact that I've opened the door to the seat *behind* the driver a million times, too. Anyway, I open the driver's door and get in, and move the seat up to account for my shorter legs, flailing with my right foot until it finds a pedal. Then I sit up straight. Gas, brake, gas. I can reach them both comfortably, so my seat is where it needs to be. I've read the manuals, I know how this works, I've just never actually had an in-car lesson before.

Dad is watching me, arm resting on my open door. He nods his encouragement, as if The Moving of the Seat is my first trial and I have passed. "What's next?" he asks.

I sit staring at the dashboard. I know this one. "Um, mirrors?"

"That's correct, Ensign," he says. As long as I can remember, we've always played spaceship when we're alone in the car together. "Go ahead."

The rearview is easy enough. I shift it until the back window is framed in it. Then I try to tackle the side mirrors. Dad closes the door so that I can see how I'm moving the one on my side. He stands in the spot where a car would be coming up on me, and waits until I have him centered. Once I'm good, he goes around to the other side and stands still for me again. Without ever having actually watched cars approach from behind me, I'm not sure I've got it exactly right, but I give it my best shot. Before he can say anything about it, I put my seatbelt on.

He heads around to the passenger side and gets in. It's weird looking at him from the other side. It feels like he should look more different, like the reverse side of a coin.

"Can I start it?" I ask once he's strapped in.

"At will, Ensign," he says.

"Aye, Captain," I say, playing along.

Turning the key is such a small part of the process of driving, but such a huge and symbolic one. I am taking control of this beast, activating it, claiming it as my familiar, or my servant, to take me where I wish to go. It roars to life, and so far it obeys me. Of course, I haven't actually asked it to do anything yet.

There's only one road, a smoothly paved path with nothing more complicated than gentle curves. The speed limit is 10. I shift into drive, add shy pressure to the gas until the car starts creeping forward, and just like that, I'm driving. Dad's right: it's the safest place in the world to learn to drive. It's not like there's any way to get lost or any reason to rush.

Until there is.

A car eases up behind me, following really close. It blinks its headlights at me. Then the road turns and I see more cars behind it.

"Is that a funeral procession?" I ask.

Dad turns around and studies the situation for a second. "Yep. Looks that way. Steady as she goes, Ensign Diaz. You're doing fine. The speed limit is the same for everyone."

I don't feel like I'm doing fine. I feel like I'm making the car jerk forward every time I try to ease onto the gas, and it's hard to know whether I'm centered on the tiny road or not. Roads are supposed to have lines on them to make them easier to follow. As easy as it was to coast a minute ago, now that I'm self-conscious it's hard to go really slow and keep everything steady. The car whines. It either wants to go for real or just stop. It doesn't want to be my snail. I feel it fighting me.

I've just about found my groove again when the car behind me does the worst thing it could possibly do: it honks the horn. It's probably actually just a little tap, but it startles me just as badly as if he'd totally leaned on it. My heart is suddenly in my throat and a chill of panic grips my spine. Reflex takes over and my foot jams down hard. On the gas.

The road turns, but the car doesn't. It rockets straight ahead, and whatever my foot thinks it's doing, it's apparently frozen in place doing it. I should turn the wheel, but I don't know where I could steer that would actually make things any better, and my hands are frozen in the same death-grip that's weighting down my feet. Dad's telling me to brake, but instinct only makes me brace myself, pushing my foot down harder. I'm used to having more time to react to things, to make decisions, and it's like I'm stuck in place. Only for a few seconds, but they're seconds I don't have. Even if I wasn't aiming right at a tombstone just off the road, there are so many that I wouldn't be able to avoid all of them, not with my brain suddenly blank on how to find the brakes. My first instinct, though that comes to me too late, too, is to shout at the stone to move.

Which is stupid, because it's rock. Not just rock, but really, *really* well anchored rock.

Wishing and hoping isn't enough to make the gravestone move out of the way. There's a weird, slow-motion kind of lurch where each second feels like it's been split into ten parts. All of those parts lead to the same inevitable thing but they tick by slowly, giving me time to absorb how thoroughly screwed up this is all about to be.

There's a scrape and a bang. I don't know which comes first, or if they both kind of happen at the same time. The impact isn't like when you play bumper cars at the county fair. Bumper cars are meant to crash repeatedly. They have rubber cushions around them. There's still a jolt when they hit each other, but they bounce off, too. This isn't like that.

Then there's a hiss and a *whoomp*, and now I'm face first into a big white cloud that fills my nose with powder and smells like a pool float being barbecued.

Then there's silence.

CHAPTER 4

"So... maybe that wasn't the best idea, after all?"

Dad's voice is the next thing I'm aware of. Even though I don't think I've passed out, I'm out of the car, sitting on the grass with a blanket wrapped around me, and Dad is next to me, dusted with white powder, gently wiping my face with a damp towel. Some amount of time has gone by in which I've moved and said things and done things, without remembering any of it. The water on the towel feels soothing, and it cools the air hitting my face, and it isn't until I feel like maybe I won't have to throw up after all that I realize I was ever queasy in the first place. A bottle of water is half-full next to me. I pick it up and take a sip.

There's a woman in a uniform kneeling beside us, and I panic that she's a cop and she's going to arrest me for property damage or something. But no, she's a paramedic, and her nametag says Leslie. I don't know if that's a first name or a last name. She's talking to me and I'm responding. It's all automatic, as if from a distance. My body is on autopilot, doing and saying the things it needs to. I wonder if Leslie can tell she's only getting the emergency backup system. This is her job; she probably can.

There are cops here, too. I see the lights flashing on a patrol car a ways down the paved lane. I don't see the funeral procession. I guess there was plenty of room to get around our car once I ran off the paved path.

My pupils, or whatever the paramedic is checking, test out fine, and she packs up her kit. There's a guy in a three-piece suit talking to the cop, down by the patrol car. Otherwise, it's just us. Dad's talking, and then he's not. Instead he's watching me like it's my turn to talk.

I lean instead, forehead to his shoulder, and he puts his arms around me. "I'm sorry," I tell him.

"I'm sorry, too," he says. "Jokes aside, I really did think it would be a nice safe place."

"Am I going to jail?"

"No, *mija*, you're not going to jail." I know he feels awful about all this because he only uses Spanish when he's really emotional.

"Am I grounded?"

"Only in the sense that you're not going to be piloting the shuttlecraft anytime soon. We can talk about the rest later."

"Are we going home?"

"Mom's coming to pick us up, and a tow truck is coming for the car."

I wince. "Is it going to be expensive?"

He hesitates, and that tells me yes. "Well, we can't drive it once the airbags deploy. You have to get new airbags put in first. The actual damage to the car, I don't know. And we'll have to pay for a new headstone. But we can talk about it all later, after we get the insurance estimate. You're still in shock."

Shock. Is that why I'm shivering and sweating at the same time?

It flits through my awareness that medicine and health are at 610 in the Dewey Decimal system. This is probably the least useful thing I could realize right now.

"No, Dad, tell me now. Otherwise I'll imagine it's way worse than it is."

He rubs my back. "No one was seriously hurt. No one's in trouble. It's just money. Now, I share some blame here, so I'm willing to pay one and you'll pay the other—of the car repair and the headstone, I mean. And then we'll get you driving lessons for real, but not until you've paid off your share."

I don't know how he can be so calm that he's thought all of this out and come up with answers already.

"Totally fair." It's definitely less bad than the bad I was braced for, so I'm relieved. And, go figure, once I'm relieved is when I start to cry.

When I start to cry is, go figure, when Mom shows up. She tells us not to get up and she crouches to hug Dad and me. She's shaking, but once she's convinced we've still got all our parts attached she relaxes a little.

"You look like you've seen a ghost," Dad says.

"You look like you *are* ghosts," she answers. I look down at my shirt, to find that I'm all covered and caked with airbag powder just like Dad is. With the bottle of water and the towel, I try to rinse out my hair. The water feels good on my scalp, but lifting my arms stirs some of the dust into the air and makes me realize my eyes are burning. I don't dare rub them with the filthy towel, so I just go back into that distant numb place and then I don't feel them so much anymore.

Dad stands and talks with Mom for a minute, then he crouches down with me again while she takes a stroll around the car to look at the damage. I haven't seen it yet, but from the way she's biting her lip I'm not sure I want to.

The cop gets back in his cruiser, and the guy in the three-piece suit starts walking toward us. With him is another guy I didn't notice before, in a black suit and a cheap tie, looking like every chauffeur I've seen on television ever.

The fancy suit guy and Dad have already met, apparently, but he introduces himself to me and says he's the manager of the cemetery. I start to get up, but all four adults—expensive suit, cheap suit, Mom, and Dad—instantly put their hands out and tell me to stay where I am. It's probably wise advice, since I'm not sure my knees would hold me if I asked them to, but it just makes me feel even smaller and more talked-down-to. Literally.

The other guy is the driver who honked at me. He says he's sorry for flustering me and he didn't mean any harm. "I assure you, I've officially told the police that you weren't speeding or being reckless. But," he glances at the manager guy, "this is a serious, somber place that people visit to be respectful of the dead, and it's not a driving course, and maybe you'll remember that in the future."

The upshot seems to be, if I don't try to claim that he disturbed the peace and drove me off the road, he won't try to claim that I was being reckless. They don't say it straight out, but that's what I get from it.

I feel sheepish while he's talking, but once they turn and walk away something flares in me. My eyes sting full-force and my hair is dripping down my back, and the grass is prickly underneath me. It's like anger has burned away the fog, because now I'm thinking that there's not much "respect for the dead" in honking your stupid horn in a graveyard, and what if we were only going slow because we were visiting someone and looking for the right plot. And—oh! We *weren't* even going too slow. We were going the speed limit. You know, *respectfully.*

I don't say any of it out loud. Not now. Even though they're far enough away that they probably wouldn't hear me mutter under my breath, I don't feel like taking that chance.

As much as I try to—and I really have tried—I have never been able to understand when people say they need to be alone. Maybe it's because I'm an only child, so "alone" has always just been the default.

Mom is an only child. She gets it. Dad comes from a big family, so when he's moody he doesn't want anyone around. I wish I could understand what that's like—wanting to be alone with your dark thoughts and fears instead of wanting to be rescued from them, so that it wouldn't feel so much like I've failed at helping when someone chooses solitude over my company. I always feel like I haven't done the right things in the right combination to unlock the safe that their happiness is trapped in. Like I'm a failure at being that companion-who-notices-your-pain that I'd want someone to be for me.

Like if I could just get them to try it my way, to let me in, it would work for them, too.

Maybe for people who aren't only-children, when you always have people crowding around and eavesdropping on your personal moments, getting time to yourself is like a magical bubble that lets you breathe. I don't know. It's beyond my experience how solitude can make things any better instead of just encouraging the downward spiral.

So when Dad retreats to the privacy of his bedroom and closes the door, a little part of me somewhere inside takes it personally.

Like it's me he's walking away from. Some of the strength goes out of me, and my eyes sting with big, burning tears.

I have my best alone-time when I'm in a room with someone else. We don't even have to be interacting much. I just need to know someone's there. Not that I'm constantly afraid that something bad is going to happen, but it's comforting to know someone would know if it did.

Mom and I are curled up at opposite ends of the couch, our feet sometimes touching in the middle, both reading on our own, and just the twitch of toes and the turning of pages or soft clicks against a touch screen are enough to tell me that I'm not completely alone. I'm pretending to read, but really I've just been staring past the same paragraph for half an hour. She glances up when I sniffle the tears back. I think she's reading. She might be playing a game on her tablet. Either way, it's comforting that she's there.

I ache all over from the accident, and the more I calm down the more I ache, which gets me upset and re-living my freeze-up and the impact and the rain of powder all over again. It's weird how it happened so slowly and so fast at the same time, and I'm already starting to doubt my memories of it. Everything's blurry except for the few slowed-down seconds that stand out in HD from the rest. I'm going over it again and again, mentally replaying it like they do with football on television. The only way it could be worse is if a team of three retired pro drivers were drawing circles on the screen and analyzing what I could have done differently.

I have medication for moments like this, when the brain weasels won't stop squeaking on their exercise wheel. It's hard to give in and take it, but I get up and go upstairs to take one now. It's a tiny pill, smaller than an pencil eraser, but it takes the edge off when it feels like the world is standing on my chest and making it hard for me to breathe.

Anxiety medicine is a tricky thing. It's something you're less likely to take if you have to ask someone to dispense it to you, but I know that my parents want to keep an eye on how I use it all the same. So we compromise. I keep it in my medicine cabinet, and once a week it's counted to see how much I've used, and if I need a refill, and all that kind of thing. I don't abuse it or give it to friends or take it when I don't need it, so I don't mind. The counting doesn't offend me. When I return to the couch, the cat is in my spot, purring up happily from my residual warmth. I scoop him up and plop him on Mom's hip. Eventually, he settles in the negative space between my leg and hers.

It doesn't seem like it's still the same day it was when I woke up this morning with Keisha and then we drove her home. It doesn't seem like a Saturday at all, so I'm surprised when Andrew turns up at the door just as twilight starts casting lavender shadows through the living room.

I know it's him because he always knocks before he rings the doorbell. I start to get up to answer it, and suddenly everything hurts and the room makes a little spin. Not a spin, exactly, but a definite dip to one side, like a funhouse hallway. I stood up like an hour ago and it was fine. Shock and stress do weird things to a body. Or maybe it's just that I haven't eaten anything substantial since morning.

"You okay to get that?" Mom asks, and I consider for a few seconds, testing myself, before I nod.

I love Andrew. I really do. But I'm not feeling up to this right now. Not the sympathy, not the explaining, and I'm definitely not going to go the route of pretending that nothing's happened so that I don't have to explain. I just want to take another dose of pain medicine, get another cup of tea, and hide under the throw blanket on the couch. If I let Mom get the door for me, I'll feel like I'm hiding from Andrew. I *want* to hide, but I feel bad about it, so I force myself not to.

Maybe I kind of understand alone time, after all.

Andrew knows something's wrong as soon as I open the door. He hugs me right there in the doorway, and shouts hello to my mom while he follows me up to my room. I'm not going out. I don't feel like being in a car again today.

He rubs my back while I tell him about it, my cheeks burning with embarrassment and shame. I'm on my stomach and nested all around by pillows, so I can't see his face. He doesn't laugh, so at least there's that, but it feels like he's holding back whatever he actually wants to say in place of the comfort-words he's giving me. Suddenly, it's important that I see his eyes.

"What is it?" I ask, squirming around till I can flop onto my back, squinting up at him. He's propped his head on his hand, elbow on the bed, looking past me rather than at me. Ice fills my stomach and creeps up my spine. "Oh, don't tell me you're dumping me. Not today. Not after all that."

Now I feel extra guilty about not having wanted to see him tonight, and horrified at the thought of never seeing him again, all because my subconscious ruined it somehow by getting flustered at a car horn in a graveyard.

He curls in on me, hugging tight. "I would never. It's okay. Don't panic, it's okay."

Never is an awfully big thing to claim, I think, and then I feel even guiltier for not feeling comforted. I'm still on my back and my eyes are welling up again, so I scrub them impatiently on his shoulder before my tears can fall and run into my ears. I stare at the dark spots of damp I've left on his shirt. "Okay, but then, what?"

"I wanted to see how you were doing after Keisha's news. She told you last night, right?"

Last night... Last night... Last night feels like it happened a year ago to a different me. I struggle to think through the fog that shrouds the night and the morning. Movie. Dinner. Giggling and fingers and tongues. Sleep. Dad's French toast. Driving her home.

Driving. I shudder.

"I don't... news?"

He gets a look on his face like he just swallowed a lizard.

She's told him something that she hasn't told me. Does this mean she trusts him more than she trusts me? And, why? What could she possibly be afraid to tell me? Does she think I'll... what?

"Well, now you have to spill it." I try to keep the tremble out of my voice, but I fail.

"Shit." He bites his lip. Where he'd gone sheet-white a moment before, now he's flushed and he looks like *he* might cry. I can see him struggling between letting her share whatever she was supposed to have told me already, and ending the agony of suspense for me. "Her dad got promoted. They're moving, over the summer."

It's that moment of impact all over again, the inevitability of knowing something's in the process of going horribly wrong and there's nothing you can do to fix it or avoid it. It's already in motion and it's going to stay that way until it crashes. Suddenly, as miserable as I was earlier in the day, I just want to be sitting in the grass again with Dad rubbing my back.

Tears are stinging behind my nose. I feel... I don't know what to feel. Stunned. Cold. Betrayed.

I can't quite get my breath, so when the words come out they're almost without sound. "Why wouldn't she tell me? Why did she tell you and not me?"

"Technically, she didn't tell me. She told Sean and he told me."

I flinch, and he feels it. "*Sean*? She told Sean and not me?"

Sean is new. Like, *new* new. Keisha and I are established. We're a serious primary-partner level relationship. At least, I thought we were. But she already knew about this last night and didn't breathe a word of it to me? She didn't even give a hint that anything was up. How good an actress is she? Fleetingly, I wonder if I've ever been able to read her at all.

He rushes onward. "But I was sure if she told him, that meant she'd already told you." He sits up, making distance, and buries his face in his hands. After a long few seconds, he combs his fingers back through his sandy hair, like he's picking his head up by the scalp. "I'm sorry. I'm so sorry. I've screwed this all up."

Anger flares hot in me. At Sean. At Ki for telling Sean. At Andrew for telling me that Ki told Sean. Some rational part of me knows that blame won't help. Blame won't change anything.

Shut up, brain, I think.

Brains are jerks.

But when the brain shuts up, I'm shunted back into the aching hollow in my chest; the hurt and the sadness, and the questions I don't have answers to.

Hearts are jerks, too.

CHAPTER 5

IMAGINE myself playing it cool. Hanging out in the library and studying together, waiting till we're curled up in my bed next weekend and saying, "So, moving's exciting. Where are you going?" She'd grasp for words and apologize and have some perfectly sensible explanation that eases everything and makes it all okay again, without making me feel even worse for having doubted her motives. Then we'd kiss and make up, and make love as if we have all the time in the world, and store up what it feels like to be in each other's arms.

That's the way it'll happen in the made-for-TV movie version. In real life, though, I leak tears all the way through work on Sunday, and then there's a Sunday night video chat where my eyes are puffy and my nose is red despite the layers of stage makeup (which Keisha taught me how to do), and the first thing out of my mouth is "What the actual hell, Ki? Why didn't you tell me?"

It's all the things I didn't want it to be: angry, accusatory, whiny. Melodramatic.

Color drains from her face. "Allie —"

"You could tell Sean, who you've been dating for like a month, but you couldn't tell me?"

Her mouth works a couple times, practicing at sounds before any come out. "It's not like that. He was over at the house and my parents were talking about it like I'd told everyone already, and he heard them."

Maybe that should make it better, but instead it just makes it worse. I don't get to hang out at her house and tell her parents that we're dating, but he does because he's a boy. I have seniority in her life, by two whole years, but he's the one who's socially accepted. He's the one she can show off. I'm a secret she thinks she can't tell anyone about. I'm reminded of that conversation with my dad after we dropped her off. He thinks her parents would be cool about it. Everyone does, except her. Suddenly, I feel like I don't matter to her at all. Why am I not important enough to tell people about?

"I was going to tell you this weekend, I swear," she insists. "But we were having so much fun and I didn't want to make everything all sad. I just wanted to enjoy the moments we have left together."

"Please, don't make it sound like you did this to spare me or something. That's crap."

She huffs. "I didn't do it *for* you. I chickened out because I'm a chicken who chickens, and I didn't know how to tell you. I didn't know how to throw it into a conversation without upsetting you."

"Yeah, well. Good job not upsetting me." I wince at my own words, but it's too late to take them back. I have to stand behind them now.

Her lips tighten into a thin line. Keisha's lips are always so full and soft that I hate seeing them distorted into something so hard and unkind. Even her lips are pushing me away. "You haven't even asked where we're moving to," she says.

I want to know. More than anything. I want to know if it's going to be within casual visiting distance, or if there's at least a direct train. If there's any way at all that we can keep our relationship going or if she's going to decide that her moving is a knife that severs us whether I want it to or not. But with the way everything's going today, this weekend, I feel like the act of asking the question will be the trigger that picks the destination, and that will make the answer a really bad one. I don't think I can take any more bad right now.

"Maybe when you're feeling *brave* enough, you can figure out how to tell me." I slam my laptop closed, dropping my connection and ending the call. Then I stare at the shelf-of-books decal on the lid and watch tears drop onto it with loud splats.

I hadn't meant to hang up on her, and I don't know why I did it. I wanted the last word, maybe, or to make a dramatic gesture, like slamming a door or whirling out of a room. If I stormed out of a room, she'd come after me and we'd talk it out. It's not like she can push my computer open from inside the chat window.

My phone buzzes. She's calling me back. I want to pick up, but I'm frozen to the spot, just like I was in the car. I feel flushed with guilt about shutting my computer and I'm still too angry to apologize for it, even though I already regret it. My hands tremble, flat on the laptop cover. If I did answer it, what would I even say?

The phone stops vibrating, so now the opportunity is lost. I feel lost, too.

I leave my phone on top of the laptop and drag my comforter downstairs to the couch. Mom and Dad are watching the news, and Brenna's in the reclining chair playing a game on her phone. Nobody watches news anymore, except my parents. I usually think it's silly that they do, but right now I'm kind of appreciating it. I huddle up in a little ball and fall asleep to the steady timbre of newscaster voices.

Keisha tries to call three times. Then she leaves three text messages. Because my phone is upstairs and I'm not, I don't see them until the morning.

"<3"

"I'm sorry."

"See you tomorrow."

I have an exam the next day so I can't stay home, but I've never been so tempted to have my parents call me in sick. After the car accident, they probably wouldn't even question it. I made it to work yesterday, but I could say that I overdid it at work; I could still be too sore today, or my eyes could still be bothering me, both of which are true.

I shuffle to the kitchen when I hear the kettle whistling, moving slowly on sore legs, building my supporting case because I haven't decided whether I'm going to play the wounded card or not. If I do, it's better to already have evidence stacked in my favor.

Dad's in the kitchen when I get there, still in a gray t-shirt and the long nylon basketball shorts he sleeps in, even though I can't imagine him ever having shot the hoops—he's like 5-foot-9. He takes in the fact that I'm not dressed yet and my hair is still a bird's nest, and he gives me a long, gentle hug. We were in the same room last night, but this is the first time we've really faced each other since we got home from the accident.

"How's your dignity feeling?"

I assume I've misheard him, or that he's using some obscure Spanish euphemism for a body part. "My what?"

"Your pride. I know it got sprained this weekend. It's a tough injury. Strange one, too: the best way to heal it is to get back out there. Every day you let yourself sit it out on the bench, it gets harder and harder to remember why you're supposed to get back in the game."

I blink. "Wait. You don't heal a sprain by running around on it. Aren't you *supposed* to rest? With ice, or something?"

He pauses, head tilted. I know he's replaying his metaphor in his head. "Yeah, fair point. It's more like… well, just work with me, here. You know what I mean, right?"

I wonder if he thinks I'm just reluctant to get back in a car, or if he knows more about everything else that's going on than I've realized. There's a certain gravity to having been in a car accident, and it's completely negated when that car accident is you hitting some random tombstone. I ache, but if I tell anyone why, they'll just laugh. It's not much different than how you can ache emotionally for someone, but if she doesn't want to let on that you're together, it's hard to express how much losing her means.

I know what he means, and I hate what he's said because I know he's right. If I hide today, I'm going to want to hide tomorrow, and I do kind of need to go back to school eventually if I want to pass eleventh grade.

"My dignity hurts a lot," I admit. I rest my head on his shoulder.

Dad ruffles my messy hair. "I know, kiddo. Why don't you go get dressed and see how it feels then?"

With only about a month left in the school year, we all know each other's schedules pretty well. That means that

Keisha expects me to go to my locker after first period, so if I want to avoid her I can just go straight to my next class and swing past my locker after second. I can take the lunch line closest to the windows, even though it's my long-held conviction that the second line from the wall has the best food. I can clamshell a second tray on top of my lunch and sneak it off to the library. I can eat in the back room where they keep the videos that teachers can check out. Technically, there's no eating in the library, but I volunteer there every day and I'm practically staff. So, all of this is what I do. The adults turn a blind eye while they eat their own lunches beside me.

While I eat, I tune out the conversation around me until I'm just aware enough to be lulled by the voices. I think about what Dad said and I wonder if this counts as hiding. It probably does. Even though I can rationalize it to myself in a dozen or so ways, I know that this isn't really about avoiding interpersonal conflict so that I can focus on my schoolwork, or getting away from crowds so that I can study, or spending more time in the library so that I can get a good recommendation letter when I'm ready to go to college. It's about not facing the fact that I was feeling hurt last night and I lashed out. Even knowing why it happened doesn't actually excuse it. That's something Brenna would say.

There's entirely too much wisdom in my life for me to be able to maintain a sulking fit for long. Maybe—another excuse—I'm studying how long a girl can hold out against sense and reason. You know, for science.

Avoiding three people is harder than avoiding one. They've got that strength in numbers thing, and they can spread out and use sneaky tactics. I'm on my guard all day, jumpy and sullen, but they all leave me alone. It's like one of those movies where the monster is unleashed but the person doesn't know where it is, and it shows up just when they're finally relaxed again, except it's brought two friends and they close in and the humans realize the monsters are intelligent and organized enough to work together strategically, and this means that humanity is doomed.

There's probably some rule somewhere about how it's not polite to compare people you're dating to velociraptors. If there is, I just broke it. I swear, I meant it as a compliment.

It's a compliment because they surround me exactly like that after school, while I'm on my shift at the public library. I'm shelving books with a volunteer girl named Paisley. They block me into an aisle, Keisha and Sean on one end of the stack and Andrew on the other. When I realize I can't get away from the three of them, mostly because I'm on the clock and can't actually leave, I suck it up and face the situation. I've known all along that I needed to do that, I just didn't know how to get myself there.

Paisley slips off down the aisle, brushing past Andrew and leaving me to my fate. Keisha doesn't look angry, and she doesn't look like she's been crying. I feel bristly about that at first, but by the time she sneaks her hand into mine the hackles have already smoothed back down.

"Allie…"

"I'm an idiot." It's important to me that I say it before she can. "I know I am. I'm sorry."

"I'm the idiot," Andrew volunteers. "I should have kept my stupid mouth closed."

"Your parents are the idiots," Sean says to Keisha, "for assuming you'd already told everyone."

"You guys, leave a little blame for Allie. She'll keep hoarding some of it in secret if we don't accept it from her." Keisha squeezes my hand. My cheeks feel feverishly hot.

When did she get to know me so well?

Andrew touches my cheek. "You two are the closest of any of us. Of course you'd take it the hardest. But, come on. We've got a couple more months of her. You wouldn't deprive me of two months of watching hot girls kiss, would you?"

Andrew is Andrew, always and foremost. At that, I laugh, and a shushing sound issues from behind the desk in return. Rather than silence me, it drives me into uncontrollable giggles.

I spend a *lot* of time in libraries. Probably more than twenty hours a week, almost every week for the last two years. I've never heard a librarian actually shush anyone before. I feel like I need a library bingo card or something, so that I can press down a big red stamp and commemorate the moment. Achievement unlocked. I gesture to Janice, the head librarian, that I'll be right back, and I head outside with one hand on Andrew's sleeve and one hand on Ki's.

Still giggling, we all head to one of the stone picnic benches in the landscaped courtyard. It hasn't rained in a few days, so the benches are dry.

"You guys are going to get me in trouble at work!"

"Well, if you hadn't tried to avoid us…" Andrew starts.

Sean finishes, "We would have been happy to get you in trouble at school instead."

Keisha and I share a look, our current situation suspended for a quick moment. They're finishing each other's sentences? Clearly there's more to their developing friendship than just the bond of men who've killed video game aliens together.

I sit on the picnic table with my feet on the bench. We're not allowed to do that, but at the moment I'm feeling giddy and a little reckless. I know. I'm such a rebel, right?

Keisha slides her hand into my hair, pulls me close with it, and kisses the breath out of me, just inches from Andrew's face. When I sneak a look, he's got his hand on Sean's shoulder like he's bracing himself to keep from falling over, and Sean is clutching at his own heart. They're not the only ones it's affecting: when her tongue makes its last flick over my lips and she lets me go, I feel a tingling head rush like when I stand up too fast.

"You were right, Andrew," I say, though my gaze is locked with Keisha's now. "It would be very, very wrong of me to deprive *you* of a couple more months of that. Will you forgive me for even entertaining the thought?"

He pretends to consider. "I don't know. Maybe. You did give me kind of a scare, back there."

"Okay," I say, and I give them each a kiss in turn. Even Sean, who I've never kissed before. His lips are soft, like Keisha's; and responsive, like kissing me matters to him. My brain doesn't know what to do with that, it only knows that I can't let myself think about it. I'm overwhelmed already. "I gotta go back in. I can't lose this job right now. Not when I have to save up for a gravestone."

Sean and Keisha look confused, but I'll let Andrew explain. I've got to get back inside.

CHAPTER 6

THREE years of high school and you've *never* cut a class?" Sean says it like I've committed some horrible sin. Like I've just admitted to kicking puppies for fun or something.

Yesterday we made up. Today I feel like I'm under attack. I don't know how to defend myself when I'm being scorned for *following* rules. This isn't a position I've ever been in before.

"Well, it's…" I start, stopping to collect my words when I hear myself stammer. I've got nothing to be ashamed of here. "I've never needed to. If I want to get out of class I just get a pass from the library."

He scoffs. "That doesn't count at all. I'm talking about leaving campus without permission."

I'm still not getting the appeal of this. "Where would I even go?"

"Anywhere!" He grins, his teeth gleaming like he's a salesman, or a shark. "You live walking distance from school."

"And one of my parents works at home," I remind him.

He's undeterred. "What about the Metro? You could hop over to DC, go to a museum… anything you wanted."

I shrug. "I'm honestly content in the library."

Sean throws his hands in the air like he's giving up on me. "You're totally incorruptible."

Finally, he laughs.

I did kind of hope this whole thing was just a thought exercise, but it's a relief to be sure. I let out tension I didn't realize my shoulders were holding. I don't like this game. I think of my anxiety medicine, in the bathroom cabinet at home. If I were to cut class now, it would be to run home and swallow a tiny pill, and then run back in time for my next class.

"I can, too, be corrupted," I answer, trying not to glance toward Andrew. "I've just got to think it's worth it. You can't tempt someone with what they already have."

"And what do you already have?"

"My own life-hack for getting out of classes I'm not in the mood for. I already have that. In comfort, and above board."

Keisha and Andrew watch our exchange silently, like we're a tennis match. They grin when I volley each serve. Just because I'm quiet and usually willing to go along with other people's ideas, doesn't mean I lack opinions. Or boundaries.

But the conversation apparently sticks with Keisha. After school, she says, "Let's ditch afternoon classes on Thursday and go into the city?"

I shrug. "Why can't we just go into the city on Saturday?"

"Because I've got stupid plans with my parents. Come on, please?"

When I hesitate, she closes off a little. I can see her eyes go distant.

"Why?" I ask. "Because Sean thinks it's cool? What exactly

do we need to go do at 1:30 in the afternoon that we can't just do after school?"

We stare at each other. "You usually follow my lead," she says finally.

"Because your lead usually makes sense," I answer. "Or you've got a plan I can trust."

"You trust my plans, but you don't trust me?" She's getting the edge to her voice, the one that's a warning. "How does that even work?"

I feel so tired, suddenly. Really? We're going to do this now?

I don't want to fight, especially over something stupid that should be so obvious that I don't even have words for it. When she lets me know she has a plan, like when Andrew took us to the mall, I know there's forethought, there's a goal, in whatever she wants to do. Something awesome or clever. Something worth seeing through. This time, it's so sudden and spontaneous, and she hasn't given me a hint that there's a plan. It's a reckless thing she wants to do for no reason I can see. It doesn't have one I *can't* see, either, if she's getting this defensive when I ask.

"You've never asked me to break a rule before," is what I say.

"You'd rather go sit in class than spend time with me before I move away?"

"That is *so* not what I said. I totally want to have time with you. I'm having time with you right now. I want all the time we can get."

"But I'm not more important than school?"

I stare. "What? No! I mean, I shouldn't be more important than school either. If that was the only way we could be together, Romeo Montague, things might be different, but that's not how it is. I don't understand this—any of this. Where is this even coming from?"

She clicks her tongue at me through her teeth—a noise of giving up. Of disgust. It wounds me somewhere deep, striking like an arrow and hurting when I breathe.

Keisha turns away. She'd probably slam her laptop closed on me if she could, but I'm here and she can't shut me out that easily.

I want her to come back. I want to stop fighting. I say the first thing my brain suggests:

"Where are you moving to?"

She stops, turns around, and stares at me. I wait and try not to fidget.

"San Diego," she says quietly.

That's far. Really far. Too far for a weekend, or a train. "And you have to go at the beginning of the summer? You could stay with—"

"Drama camp," she says, cutting me off. "I have drama camp at the local college. It's tough to get in, but I got in. So," she shrugs, "I've got to be there."

If she's got an answer for everything, why am I even trying? I decide to try one more time to keep her talking to me, but before I can congratulate her and ask about drama camp, she says, "I gotta go."

And then she goes, without waiting for a response.

Brenna picks me up from work. I'm still pensive and peeved, and she can tell from the moment I step outside.

"How can I help?" she asks, first thing, when I get into the car.

I think about it. Make Keisha stay? Make her talk to me? But Brenna doesn't have the power to do either of those things. "I'm not ready to go home just yet."

"I'm craving a milkshake," Brenna says. "Want to join me?" That sounds perfect, and I tell her so.

Brenna drives to the old-fashioned soda fountain, where we sit at a little table and peruse a huge menu of flavors and combinations.

"San Diego," I say over our salted caramel milkshakes when they arrive. I haven't given her any context, I realize suddenly, but with all that's been going on she knows what I mean.

"Keisha's dad being transferred from the Pentagon?" she asks.

"I guess so. He got promoted. They're moving right after finals, so we only have a couple more weeks." There's not much farther away you can go from the mid-Atlantic and still be in the continental United States. She'll be three time zones away. We'll still have video chat and texting and stuff, but it's not the same.

"Maybe you can visit her over the summer," she suggests.

I shake my head. I've been thinking this through. Honestly, I've been doing nothing but. "I can't get away from work for that long, or afford a plane ticket, until the car accident is paid for. Dad hasn't said much about any of the car stuff yet, so I haven't had to deal with it, but it's lurking. As soon as the insurance quotes come back, it's going to be front and center."

"I'm sure someone could manage to help you out," she says. Hinting, obviously, that she'll help me if I ask.

It's a relief to know there's a way if I need one, but I shake my head. "Besides, Keisha doesn't want to come out to her parents, and I don't think I could spend a whole week with her in front of her family—I can't imagine living under an illusion of being 'just friends' without needing to break it somehow. Not when she means so much to me. I hate that it's safer to stay home and miss her like crazy, but like I'd said to Dad, it's got to be her decision. I'd hate it even more if I accidentally got her caught."

"You're a martyr," Brenna says, pointing her spoon at me.

"How am I a martyr?" I've heard the word, I know what it means, but I don't know what she means by it.

"A martyr is someone who dies for their cause. That is, they sacrifice themselves for what they believe in. So, in this case, someone who denies themselves what they want in order to make things easier for someone else."

"That… seems kind of noble," I say.

"Yeah, it started out that way. Historically, I mean. Jesus was a martyr, dying for the sins of the people. But it's also been twisted around into a prideful thing. When someone's called a martyr because they're being prideful, it's an insult—like they want bonus points for their self-inflicted suffering, and it's more for attention than to really make it easier for someone else at all."

She tells me about separation anxiety, too. And how it's tempting to sabotage something you care about because it's easier to be mad than to feel helpless. It's like all those books where the kid is trying to get the beloved dog to quit following him into danger, so he says, "Go away, stupid dog, I never liked you anyway," but he's crying and dogs don't know English, so it's pretty transparent. At least to the dog. And the reader. The places that give out medals for books, though, seem to fall for it every time.

Maybe that's not the best example, but I know what she means. I was so close to breaking up with Keisha because I didn't want to think about how sad the next two months would be. Maybe I was trying to pick a fight that night on video chat, so that it would be over cleanly instead of building up to a lot of sadness and things I can't control.

Maybe. Not on purpose, though.

I don't think I'm being a martyr. I don't think I'm punishing Ki for not wanting to own up to the fact that we're together. I think I'm genuinely afraid of accidentally messing things up for her with her parents, and then leaving her behind to clean up the mess by herself while I get to go back home to my nice queer-friendly life. That's what I don't want to do. I don't know if she understands, but she says she does. Part of her isn't happy, but then there's this gratitude in her eyes that sneaks through, too. I think she's probably just as torn as I am. She probably wants more time together, too, but I'm guessing she doesn't see how we can make it work either if we're under her parents' eyes all the time.

But at least we should have the conversation, right? That's what grown-ups do. They talk it out instead of assuming or hiding or making your partners go all velociraptor on you.

Velociraptors vs Martyrs sounds like a game Andrew and Sean would play. I tell Brenna as much. It makes her happy. Later, when I text them about it, it makes Keisha and Andrew happy too. Keisha says Joan of Arc would seriously kick some dinosaur ass. And she apologizes for being bristly earlier, and agrees: we need to talk.

We decide on video chat, rather than waiting until Friday night to talk face to face. I can see her room behind her, decorated with theatre playbills from shows she's gone to, and shows she's been in. She looks tired. Her hair is natural and pulled back into a loose ponytail. In the small window-in-window I can see that mine is flying everywhere—a medusa of curls—but I don't try to tame it.

"Hey. So, I can't come over this Friday," she starts. "I'm going to my grandparents'. They're taking me to a play and whatever, while my parents go out west for the weekend to do some logistics stuff."

"Okay." My heart sinks a little, but I nod. "Thanks for letting me know. Have fun, okay?"

She laughs. "Yeah, I'll try. It'll be a house full of aunts and uncles and cousins all weekend. I won't even have my own room to escape to. But it'll be good to see them before we go, I guess."

Yeah. There it is. The going.

"Wouldn't next weekend make more sense, with Memorial Day?"

"Three day weekend and everything," she agrees. "But they've got to do bank stuff out west, and banks are closed for the holiday."

Oh. Right. The library will be open, so I forgot. "And then study week. Are you ready?" I ask.

"For school to be over? Kinda. For all the rest—finals and moving and stuff? No way."

She tells me a little about her drama camp, and the high school her parents have picked for her. I tell her about the five-day work weeks I'll be starting as soon as school is out, in order to pay for the gravestone. It's all just small talk, because neither of us wants to hang up and do homework, but it's good talk. Non-bristly talk. Then her phone, beside her computer, buzzes and beeps. She looks down at it, and then back to me with apology in her eyes. "It's my grandma. I've got to—"

"It's okay," I assure her. "See you in the morning?"

"Sure thing." She blows me a kiss and disconnects, already bringing the phone to her ear with a warm smile for the person on the other end.

The sudden silence is too loud in my ears. I put some music on to cover it, and open my history textbook, but I'm not focusing on the page in front of me. I'm thinking about what I'll do to fill the void of a Friday night without Keisha, and how many Keisha-less Friday nights I have ahead of me.

My phone buzzes. It's Ki.

"Hey. What's up?"

I hear her sigh before I hear her speak. "I'm sorry. I'm a chicken who chickens. I'm not going to my grandparents. Sean invited me out to a show, and Friday's the only time he could get discounted seats. I know it's our night, and I didn't want to seem like I was prioritizing him over you, so I panicked and lied. I'm a jerk."

He couldn't find a matinee to cut class for? I think to myself, but I don't say it. "You're not a jerk," I assure her instead. Talking just felt so good between us, and pushing my feelings aside is a small price to pay if it keeps that communication going. "You owned up within, like, minutes. That means that being a jerk isn't in your nature and you knew it didn't work for you."

"I shouldn't have tried," she argues.

"It's okay to miss a Friday, you know. Just because we have a Friday thing doesn't mean we can't be flexible sometimes. Hey, I'll see if Andrew can switch nights with you, and we could have our date night Saturday. Would that work?"

There's silence on the line. It's either an "I can't believe you're so cool with it" silence or a "there's more" silence, but I can't tell which it is. My stomach scoots to the edge of my abdominal cavity, like it's getting ready to drop.

"Um…"

So it's a "there's more." I head it off at the pass.

"So, what about the next weekend, then? That's Memorial

Day. Maybe we could spend the whole weekend together, studying and not-studying?"

"That would be awesome," she blurts, gratitude clear in her quick breath. "Thank you so much. You're the best girlfriend ever and I'm totally a jerk." I hear her mother's voice in the background, calling for her. "Okay. Gotta go for real. See you in the morning!"

She's a tsunami and I feel like the ocean floor, all churned up and exposed in her wake.

It's important to me to be the "cool with it" girlfriend. I'm the one with these awesome role models, so I'm the one who's supposed to be the pro at having multiple relationships. Sometimes this means that how I react on the outside doesn't match how I feel on the inside. This is one of those times. I told Keisha what I thought she needed to hear, not how it made me feel.

Her parents probably really *are* going away all weekend, and she's probably taking the opportunity to have an overnight with Sean like the kind she can have with me, and for some reason she can't come out and tell me.

I'm getting the feeling lately that her knee-jerk reaction is to assume she can't trust me with things. That hurts a lot. I figure if I don't react badly maybe she'll realize she doesn't have to cover things up, or tell me lies she thinks I'll find more palatable than the truth.

I'm upset at being pre-empted, of course, but I won't tell her that. Things happen and schedules change, and it's more Sean's fault for knowing it was "my" night and asking her out anyway.

No, I can't keep my "cool with it" thing going just by shifting the blame. That's the opposite of being cool with it. And I get to have her for a whole three-day weekend as a result, so really, I'm getting the better part of this deal. Right after the Memorial Day holiday, exam prep week starts. It'll be non-stop studying and review sessions, then a steep slide through exams and then she'll be leaving. Having a little oasis together before all that chaos starts will be a really good thing. I can deal with my hurt feelings on my own; it's better than antagonizing her and not being able to enjoy what little time we have left.

On the couch later, reading with Mom, I ask her about long-distance relationships. "Is it hard with Tina in Chicago and you out here? Is it harder than when she was nearby?"

She dog-ears the page to hold her place—it makes me cringe every time, but I've stopped trying to say anything about it—and looks up at me. "In some ways, it's harder. In other ways, it's easier."

That's honest, which I appreciate, but it's not very helpful, nor is it the reassuring answer I was expecting. I shiver and pull the afghan up from where it's pooled on my feet, drawing it up under my chin. In moments, Ozone is mushing his paws on me, like the blanket is a big "cat wanted" sign or something. He's purring and warm, and comforting exactly the way I wanted the blanket to be, so I let him stay and start rubbing his ears. "How can far away be easier?"

Mom has a matter-of-factness about her that's usually really calming. She's always even-tempered, in control. Right now, that makes me feel worse. Maybe it's not that *she* makes this relationship stuff look easy. Maybe it just is easy, and here I am still screwing it up.

"Now that we're long distance, visits are more expensive and they take a lot of planning. But when we do visit, we get a big chunk of concentrated time together. It's like…

like seeing Ki every day at school for a month, or spending a three-day weekend with her at the beach. The month is longer, and you can make plans last-minute, but she's got rehearsals and you've got work. There's other stuff going on for both of you. The beach is only a weekend, but it might work out to be more time together."

I nod slowly while I take that in. "Okay. But how do you keep things going in between the visits?"

Her eyes don't exactly fog right up like a car window, but they get a little shiny and downcast.

"That's harder?" I prompt her.

"Sometimes. But also, when you're out experiencing different things than each other every day, you end up having more to talk about, not less."

That sounds too good to be true.

"Then why is it so hard when my grandparents ask me what's new?"

"Because that's what happens if you wait too long. Then there's too much stuff and it all blends together. The individual pieces stop standing out."

I pretend not to hear the veiled you-don't-call-your-grandparents-enough message, just like I always do.

"So, like, a video call once or twice a week?"

"At first, maybe. Then you'll see what's more comfortable for everyone." Her voice catches when she says it. It's just a little hitch, but it changes everything from "all-knowing" mode to "softening the blow."

"You don't think we'll be able to keep it going."

She gives me a little credit by not trying to deny it. "You're a serious girl. Ki's more flighty. I don't mean that in a bad way. Just, I think the things actually in front of her tend to hold her attention better than the things that aren't. She…

You know. She likes to experience things with you, not do things and tell you about them."

"But you just said telling each other about things is how we make this work." I've stopped petting Ozone, who head-bumps at my hand to get my attention. Combing my fingers through his long fur and watching the trails they make there is easier than meeting Mom's eyes, but I look at her anyway. The bridge of my nose is stinging. Pre-tears that haven't made it to their little ducts yet.

"I did. And you'll try that for a while, but it might not work for her. And if that happens, you'll adapt and try something else."

"So you're not saying we can't last. You're saying how we talk might change. How we work might be different than how you and Tina work. Okay." I lean back and close my eyes. Mom squeezes my foot.

"We'll upgrade our data plan. Maybe sending lots of pictures will help make it feel like you're a part of what the other one is doing."

That sounds kind of fun. Taking random shots, getting random shots. Giving us things to talk about. It still doesn't help with the visiting, but it's a start. It's a way to keep involved in each other's lives.

"I'll suggest that. Thanks."

"Do you know if she has plans for the summer?"

"Yeah. Some kind of drama intensive. It's for high school kids, but it's at the community college. She'll get to meet some Drama Club people from her new school, so she won't be all alone when she gets there. She was telling me about it a little."

"Oh! That's thoughtful, huh?"

"Yeah." It comes out more sullenly than I mean it to.

"Yeah, but?" Mom asks.

"Yeah, but it's just bait to lure her out there. Come to California, we have shiny drama things."

"Like a bribe?"

"Exactly like a bribe."

"You think they're bribing her away from you?"

I don't think that. They don't even know about us.

Or, I *didn't* think that, but there's a certain resonance about it when she says it. They might not know we're dating, but they know she spends a lot of time with me when she *could* be dating. Still… "No, no. Just, you know, to get her excited about moving."

That's all.

CHAPTER 7

B Y Friday afternoon of hell week, I'm feeling prepared for whatever finals will bring. Otherwise, though, things are… tense. There are two Keishas now: the friendly one and the aloof one. When she wasn't dating anyone else, I didn't notice it, but now that she's with Sean too, and I see how public and cozy she's willing to be with him, the fact that she's in the closet about me hurts more than it ever did before.

Like, when we're all hanging out and we say goodbye. If we're in public, she moves her face deliberately away from mine so that I can't kiss her in front of anyone. Sean sees it and frowns with me, and he hugs her without kissing her. I appreciate the gesture, even though I didn't ask him to look out for my feelings and I don't think it should be his job to keep things equal. I think it should be hers.

And she's super touchy. Each time I see her, I never know whether I'm going to get the Keisha who talks to me, or the Keisha who talks to everyone *but* me. It's exhausting, keeping myself happy and calm and non-confrontational on the outside when I don't know what I'm about to face. I think about my mom and our talk, and I wonder if it gets easier.

But it's not like I'm the only one without an instruction manual for all of this. She doesn't want to move, she's hurt and confused, and we're both dealing with it badly in our own defective ways. Maybe she can tell I'm harboring a little resentment about losing a date night, and she's waiting for me to lash out. I've made peace with it, but she can't know that. Or maybe she wants me to be upset, because being upset shows that I'll miss her.

It's like death by a million bee stings. Toxins building up from every little individual jab until something that would be tiny on its own becomes a part of something that's huge and, well, toxic.

Add my period and a killer bout of cramps, and there's a chance I'm overreacting to the small stings, too. Knowing that doesn't make it any easier to change my feelings, though.

Ki turns up at my locker after school. I've accumulated a lot of junk in there—old papers, random gloves I assumed I lost over the winter, and stuff—and I figure if I shove as much as I can into my backpack each day, I won't be stuck with an insurmountable mess on the day we have to clean them out for real.

"Hey," she says.

"Hi." I know this was our planned long weekend, but it's been so touch and go that I don't ask if she wants to come home with me. I don't know what's safe to say.

At first she just watches me, smirking a little. It makes me self-conscious, but it also makes me want to laugh.

"It's just," she says, once my backpack is so full I'm really having to work at compacting the stuff in it, "it's just… it looks like you're the worst shoplifter ever."

I laugh weakly. "Yeah, I've already caught myself."

"Here," she says, "annex." She unslings her bag and sets it down next to mine, then unzips it. It's a girlfriendly thing to do. It gives me a little hope.

I hand her a stack of five spiral notebooks. She slides them into her bag. "*That* experiment failed," she notes.

I'd started the semester determined to keep each class's notes separate in their own notebooks, but that plan hadn't lasted a week. She remembers it, though. It's such a stupid little thing, but it makes my chest feel full.

She shoulder-bumps me. "You're cute when you blush. Come on."

She waits for me to zip my backpack closed and watches me stagger under the weight of it when it hits my shoulder. Then we start walking side by side like always. I guess she's still coming over. I'm kind of relieved by that and kind of scared. Can we go a whole night without setting each other off? At this point, I don't even know.

Out the door and down the street in silence. We're at the first crosswalk when she asks me what I'm thinking about.

"The solar system," I say. Not *losing you*. "My Very Educated Mastiff can Just See Under-Neath."

She blinks. I guess she's never heard that one before. "That makes no sense."

"My dad says it used to be Under-Neath Pianos, but now since Pluto's not a thing anymore…"

"It's still a thing enough to have a name. And moons. It's not like they can just decide it doesn't have moons anymore." Ki glances around quickly. "I expect Andrew to pop out of the landscaping with a comment about whether we moon Pluto or Pluto moons us."

I giggle. I can't help it. And I know better than to think that one laugh means everything's okay, but it means that she's trying to make everything okay, and that's more than I could have asked for.

Once we're off the main road, I take both her hands in mine and step back, so that we're at arm's length. "You're Pluto and I'm Charon," I say, and start to move in a circle. She moves with me. "We're tidally locked. We see each other's same faces all the time. And because we're so close in size and mass, neither of us rotates around each other. We both move together, because the center of our gravity is actually between us. It doesn't belong to one or the other of us."

Keisha closes the distance and kisses me, briefly. "That's kind of awesome. Is it true, or are you being poetic?"

"It's true. I did a report on it."

We part, reluctantly, but she slips her hand into mine when we start walking again. "Us—our relationship—is bigger than either one of us. How far apart are Pluto and Charon? It's got to be more than a couple thousand miles."

"And they do okay," I agree. "Even through all the drama and bullshit, and even being demoted from planethood."

She squeezes my hand and we walk along in silence for a while. Maybe I should have done this locker thing in two trips. My shoulder is starting to ache.

"They'll be keeping me busy, it turns out," she says. "They think if they keep me too busy to miss you guys, and too busy to have anyone out to visit, I'll adjust faster."

"It… sounds good on paper," I say, but I'm reaching.

"But?"

"But I kinda want to be missed."

She makes a little squirrel chirp noise in her throat and tugs at my hand, pulling me to another stop and into a hug right there on the sidewalk. I burrow into the scent of her like I'm trying to memorize it. When I sniffle is when she pulls back.

"We need to talk," she says, and I nod, relieved that she's the one to say it first, like wanting to be missed is the key thing she's been waiting to hear. "But here's the rule: no crying. If one of us is about to start leaking the feels from our eye sockets, we stop and do something else till we're calm enough to go on."

"Fair. But just so you know, it's probably going to take a lot longer that way."

"Oh, I know. That's okay. We have all night."

It's almost harder when things are good. All I can think about is how soon I'm going to lose her. When it's tense, I think maybe it's just as well she's moving away; maybe it's for the best. When it's good, there's something to ruin. Even if the distance doesn't screw it up, the wrong word might. I'm good at the wrong word. If there was a foot-in-mouth curriculum, I'd test into AP. And then get myself kicked out of it by saying something stupid.

I think the silence holds so heavily over us because we know we have weighty things to talk about. They aren't "hold hands and stroll" things. They're "hug a pillow and avoid eye contact" things.

Ozone is lounging across the pillows on my bed. We wake him from his catnap by putting our stuff down and getting settled. He makes the rounds, inspecting our backpacks for interesting smells. I turn the pillows over, hiding the angora layer he's left on them. When we're seated, he hops back up on the bed and shamelessly claims Keisha's lap. "Hello, traitor," she says, petting him. It's true—he much prefers to cuddle with guests. He'll always pick a visitor over someone who actually lives here.

"So, drama camp. Tell me about it?" I keep my tone light, interested. Eggshells crack underneath us all the same—she stiffens. I'm all ready for her to snap at me that she doesn't know about it because it hasn't started yet. I can *see* her winding up for it. Then she takes a breath and spins herself back down. We're both trying.

"It's a lot of acting class exercises. You get paired off to do scenes, and then there's a play everyone does, from the audition through the show. I don't know which play, but it looks like it's always an ensemble piece, so that every part is about equal."

"That sounds intense. Exciting. Do you think it might lead to some community theater?"

"That's the hope," she agrees.

"My mom suggested we text each other a lot of pictures, so we keep each other involved." I run Ozone's floofy tail through my fingers, keeping my hands busy. "But I'll understand if you can't drag your phone out in class or at rehearsals and stuff."

"No, that sounds good. But you have to send me adorable pictures of children's books and story time, and this purr-beast."

"It's a deal."

I've tried to give the conversation CPR but it trails off to nothing once I stop actively doing all the breathing for it. It's her turn to work the respirator. I wait, but we're both still just messing with the cat, studiously avoiding touching hands. He's a big cat, but he's not so big that our hands wouldn't brush.

I wish she'd say something, even if it's not something I want to hear. Just… something. But it's hard to play a game, even a spite game, with someone who doesn't know they're playing. That's what I'm doing. I'm making up rules for her and not telling her what they are.

I cave. I lose. Whatever. I speak first, trying again.

"Is there—" I start, at the same time that she says "I'm not—"

We both stop, and Ozone mrows into the silence. We've both slacked off on our cat-petting.

"I'm not sure how late you want me to stay tomorrow, but they're going to be packing all day so it's fine if I'm here, out of the way."

That's an overture, unmistakably. We'd talked about having the whole weekend, and she's forgotten, but she's trying. I feel my spine soften, a little less tense. "Sure. It's supposed to be nice out, if you want to go do something."

"The pop-up carnival is back, next to the farmers' market. We could go on the whirly-thing all day and see who gets sick first."

I snerk under my breath. She got sick first, last time, and she's reminding me of it on purpose. "To be fair, you didn't know you had the flu."

"I still spatter-painted you and half the town."

"It was only clothes. Clothes come off."

"Is that a fact?" she asks archly, and gives my door a pointed look.

Whoa. I wasn't expecting things to turn down this road this fast. "From vomit to sex? Andrew? Is that you?"

"Maybe Andrew's on to something."

Maybe she's changing the conversation because she doesn't want to cry—that was her rule, after all. Maybe she's delaying it because she doesn't know what to say. Maybe she just wants touch, and there's no ulterior motive behind it.

She shifts, displacing Ozone, and pulls her shirt off. Suddenly, reasons don't much matter.

We remember to put clothes on sometime before morning. Cuddled together, overwhelmed with love, as the light outside the window turns luminous dusty blue, feeling as raw and exposed as I can imagine ever feeling, I finally manage to whisper, "I'm going to miss you so much." My voice only cracks a little.

She holds me fiercely. "I know that. Do you think I don't know that? I can't even imagine being so far away from you." She sighs. "This whole moving thing has been so screwed up. You have no idea."

It's true, I don't, but it's not like that's *my* fault. Breathing deeply, I wait out my surge of frustration.

We don't try to avoid eye contact. We don't try to hold back tears, not even to satisfy a rule she's forgotten having made yesterday, so I don't remind her of it. She's talking, finally. *We're* talking. Like us, not like the angry, guarded people who have been standing in as our understudies because we haven't wanted to deal.

"So, tell me how screwed up it's been," I say, once I'm sure I can say it gently.

"I hadn't told you because it wasn't definite yet. I was trying not to hurt you. And then my parents announced it in front of Sean and he was upset, and I was upset, and then he went to blow off steam and kill aliens with Andrew before I realized I should have asked him not to say anything. And you were mad, and you were right. I've been trying to balance everyone's feelings and I've been awful at it. You've been doing this dating-two-people thing a lot longer than I have. It's hard to— Well, there's a difference between being equal and being fair. And knowing when's the right time to be which."

"I was so busy being hurt, I didn't think about how hard this was on you," I admit. "That's not fair. But you can be out about dating Sean in ways you can't be out about dating me, and I feel like that makes things automatically unequal and unfair."

"I know," she says gently. "But we've always had your house, and that was always enough, until Sean. I get to do a lot of things with you that I don't do with him. Like sleep a whole night together. Even if I was out to my parents, if they knew we were dating, we'd have to sit on the couch without touching, and have quiet awkward dinners, and we'd have to go out just to be able to hold hands. Best case scenario, those are the achievements we'd unlock."

"I know," I echo. She's good at making that thing I feel jealous over sound like something that isn't worth jealousy at all. I find the comfort she's trying to give me, and I take it.

"I *never* talk back to my parents, but I told them they'd ruined everything for me. I didn't know how to look at any of you. I didn't know how I was going to make us work. I looked into my college fund, and how much I'd screw future-me if I took a loan out against it, if I came out to them and they kicked me out. I didn't go that far, but I… I might have threatened to stay here and move in with you, and not go at all. They came up with drama camp as an apology for making me move. They thought fast."

I squeeze her. This is a bigger mess than I realized, much bigger than just the two of us. I'd had no idea how much thought and calculation she'd put into it and how upset the news had made her. "You could still… stay here. If you want."

She kisses me. Her lips are soft and only a little bit quivery. "I know. One word to your parents and they'd already have started making room for my stuff. It's so tempting. God. But they're my family too, and it's only a year and then I move out and go wherever I want. We can apply to the same colleges, you and me, and live together legitimately, for real."

"Mmm. Just a year off, and then back to our plan-in-progress?" I ask, and she nods.

That sounds amazing. What I don't say—what *we* don't say—is that our relationship has to survive that year first. If the last few weeks are any indication, that's going to mean a lot of work. Are we up to it? I don't know. Only if we're both trying at the same time.

We decide officially that we're not going to have a set good-bye. It'll be too hard. Whichever time happens to be the last time we see each other before moving day, that'll be it. We'll still have phone and text and video chat.

I expect my anxiety to totally kill me at just the thought of it, but oddly, I'm okay. We've made our peace and everything's sweet. If it's good-bye then it's good-bye on the right terms, and if it's not, then the next time is a gift.

That's the outside face. No promises that I won't obsess on it in private. But it *is* kind of a relief to know there probably won't be a tearful scene. I hate crying in public, even if it seems like I don't, for how much I've been doing it lately.

"Is the packing mostly done?" Mom asks over breakfast—eggs, grilled tomatoes, beans, and toast.

"The government is doing it. You should see it. It's fast, efficient, and it's completely weird watching strangers handling all your things. Everything that isn't nailed down has been boxed, with no thought to content or common sense. We have to hide our essentials and garbage to keep those from getting packed too. We'll already be unpacking a whole unopened six-pack of packing tape when we get to the new house, for all the good it will do us then."

"Are you having a party or anything before you go?" Brenna asks.

"I think it would be way awkward," Keisha answers. "People celebrating because I'm leaving?" She smirks and I poke her lightly with my elbow.

"Martyr," I say under my breath.

"Velociraptor," she corrects me. "No, I don't want to think of it as *leaving*-leaving. It's boarding school for a year, and then I'll be back for college—UVA or University of Maryland, or I'll convince Allie to apply out west. And we'll be back for winter break. Carl's getting married at Christmas."

My first bitter thought is that Sean will be her plus-one to her brother's wedding, not me. My second bitter thought is that if her whole family is here then we'll have to sneak around them like always.

Brenna and Mom are both watching the tiny storms that gust across my face.

"Well, maybe you can stay here over break," Mom says.

I steal a glance at Keisha, who's stealing a glance at me. We have allies, at least, and that's worth a lot. If I don't get to go to the wedding, I'd at least get the rest of the break with her, in a safe space where we can be ourselves.

"It's okay to have anger." Brenna is a licensed therapist. She says things like this all day. "It means you're afraid, and being afraid means that you care. Specific thoughts show you what specific things you're afraid of. Just, there's a difference between having an angry thought and being angry. Don't be angry. Use the thoughts to identify the concerns and then talk them out."

I'm feeling a little skewered by the psychology lesson, but I have to admit she has a point. The worst-case thought is my go-to. Instead of getting bogged down in feeling guilty about that, maybe I can say "I know it's stupid, but this is my big fear." Then either we can laugh about it and defuse it, or she can say "that's not stupid" and I'll know it's a valid concern. Either way, there'd be less stewing than is happening now.

Like at the library. Checking books in when they haven't been checked out is kind of pointless and annoying, but the more books we check in, the more we can show the county that people are using the library. It's hard to be annoyed when every beep is justifying my next paycheck. Brenna calls this "reframing the narrative." Taking the same facts and looking at them differently.

I'm not hungry anymore, and the coffee tastes bitter no matter how much I doctor it up. I sigh and push my chair back. "Okay. I need a shower," I say. "You kids talk amongst yourselves."

Dad, who's been quiet this whole time, watches me go.

"So, have you ever been to San Diego?" I hear Keisha ask my parents as I head toward the stairs. They have, it turns out, and by the time I hit the threshold of my room, Dad is listing off cool places and Brenna's coming up the stairs saying something about a photo album.

I loop a towel over my arm and wait, and in a moment there's a tap on my open door.

"Come in."

"You okay?" Brenna asks from the doorway.

"Yeah. I just need a minute. And also I stink."

"Okay. She's just scared too, you know. Come laugh at old pictures of your parents when you're ready."

"I know." I hoist my towel like I'm about to get down to business with it, and manage a grateful smile before she leaves to rummage for her photos.

My favorite part is after the shower, after you think you've dried off really well, when you open the bathroom door and step out of the steamy air into the regular, air-temperature air. That shock of cool is super refreshing.

When I get out of the shower, Keisha is on my bed, dressed for the day. I'm in a terrycloth bathrobe with a towel around my hair. I untuck it and let it drape on my shoulders like a shawl. I'm in that cool air euphoria headrush place. There's a chance the water was maybe a little too hot, but it felt good to scrub everything away.

"So? How were my parents in their dorky youth?"

Ki laughs. "They weren't so bad. My dad had a 'fro."

I can't imagine Commander Harris, who looks like the scary drill sergeant character in every movie ever, with a big afro. "Nuh-uh."

"I swear! I'll send you proof once we unpack it."

Maybe the reminder that she's moving should tense me up again, but it doesn't. She says it casually. No eggshells.

"Your first photography assignment," I agree.

"Okay. You're on. Your first assignment is… hm. Every morning, take a mirror selfie, full length, of what you're wearing for the day."

Keisha, if I haven't said it lately, is pretty smart. "Okay, but you have to do it, too."

She nods. "Deal. Starting the day I get to California."

I get fluttery in my stomach. We have a plan. We're going to try to stay connected. For the first time I feel actual hope that we can make this work. "Well… cool."

"So, why the sudden need for clean? That wasn't random."

I pull a sundress out of my closet and slip it on over my head, moving towel and robe out of the way as I go. I'm totally stalling and she knows it, but she's patient with me.

"It's just…" The dress is black with huge pink and red roses on it. I drape the damp stuff over my desk chair and go to the dresser for a pair of tights.

"Just… ?"

"Sorry." I smirk. "I didn't get much sleep."

She doesn't look the slightest bit sorry about that. A nod prompts me onward. "And?"

"And I'm pre-menstrual and a little punchy, and sometimes it feels like my parents have it all figured out, but they only share the right answers when they feel like it. Usually not till after we've screwed up. It's like they're sitting there watching our train wreck with these nostalgic 'remember when we were stupid' smiles on their faces. I mean, I appreciate they're trying to help, but sometimes it's annoying the way they do it." I pull my tights up sharply over my hips. I feel my fingernail go through before I hear the nylon rip. I could take them off, but trying again with a new pair probably won't end up going any better.

By the time I can mutter "damn it," Keisha's already at my shelf and picking out the clear nail polish. She makes me sit still while she takes care of the little run for me. A dab of polish at each end, to keep it from spreading. She blows the polish dry, tests it with her finger, and then touches her lips to the gap, kissing it better.

"They frustrate you. I know. How do you think you could change that?" Ki asks.

"You're channeling Brenna."

"Brenna would tell you that if you talked to them sooner, not just when things hit the fan, they'd be able to help earlier. They can't know what you don't tell them."

"I'm surprised you're being the advocate for keeping parents in the loop," I say, and it's honest; without venom. I wouldn't have been able to make it come out that way yesterday even if I tried.

Ki rests her head on my thigh. "I'm so jealous that you *can* talk to your parents. You grew up with this, so I don't think you see how huge it is that they're cool with it. I wish I could be open with my parents like you can."

"Am I being an entitled brat?"

She gives my thigh a squeeze. "No. You're being punchy because your girlfriend is moving and you didn't get much sleep, and someone ruined your new tights."

"They're not —"

Before I can even finish, she hooks a finger in the hole she just repaired, and she pulls. The pressure on the glued seam gives some resistance, but it pops without much trouble. A ladder of unraveled nylon opens all the way down my leg.

"Oops," she deadpans. "Here, I'll help."

She proceeds to kiss the rip all better, pausing only to make sure she's closed the door. This constant-arousal thing is new and a little surprising. Maybe it's how she's dealing with how little time we have left.

We go to the carnival. When she kisses me, I taste myself on her lips.

CHAPTER 8

GET my period right at the end of the month, the weekend before exam week. It's hard to focus on finals with Keisha moving, cramps taking up my attention, waiting for the statement from the car accident to come in… everything that's going on. I'm good at taking tests so I've got that in my favor, at least, but I'm still juggling a lot of things: studying, work, seeing Keisha as much as possible, making time for Andrew, house chores, and, you know, sleep. As a result, finals week is mostly a blur of highlighter, blue books, and multiple-choice bubbles. At least my flow is light and I'm over it by Tuesday. We hang out as a foursome, cuddling while we study, each in our own world with our headphones feeding us our own environments.

Andrew likes movie soundtracks. I have an app that sounds like the ambient background noise in a coffee shop. Keisha studies to New Agey spa music. This much I already knew. When I offer to trade an earbud with Sean, I'm expecting metal. I'm surprised to hear classical piano instead. It works well with the murmur-and-clink of my virtual café, so I keep it in for a while.

The spring concert counted as the final exam for chorus, so Ki and I are done a day earlier than everyone else. I've brought my laptop in with me in case I get bored, but the library keeps me busy. The school library has amnesty days all through finals week—bring in your overdue books and you won't get punished or fined—so I'm in the library clearing the sins from the records of the repentant when I get Keisha's text: "And we're off." It's accompanied by a little image of a person on a racehorse.

I text back a big row of hearts. They're watery by the time I hit send, but I take a big breath, wipe my eyes, and think about Dewey decimals instead. It doesn't really help. All that helps is reminding myself that it's not good-bye. It's temporary.

Sean texts me a hug a few minutes later. I return it. He sends me a little image of a book, followed by a question mark. "Yup," I reply in kind. It's easier for me to type two letters (autocomplete fills in the last one) than search for the right image. Even though technically it's the last day and no one cares, I still don't want to get busted for texting. Ki, on the road, has no such restrictions, and it makes my heart lift when I feel my phone buzz in my pocket with each new message.

Seventh period exams let out around lunchtime. Andrew and Sean show up a few minutes after the last bell of the school year rings. There are hugs all around, followed by some awkward silence while we wait out the rowdy throngs of new summer vacationers filling the hallway.

"We were gonna go to my place and play video games," Andrew says. "If you want to hang with us, we can do something else."

I punch his arm, not hard. "What, because girls don't like killing aliens? Defending the planet is my responsibility too, you know."

He looks sheepish. Before Sean, before the car incident, and before the whole mess with Keisha moving, we used to kill aliens together all the time.

"SR4?" *Swift Retaliation* is our game of choice. For one thing, the female characters actually wear armor that protects them and doesn't jiggle. Sean looks a little bemused, but mostly in a "give Andrew a hard time for it later" way.

"Maybe we can get Sean his epic blaster?" Andrew says. "You need three people for that."

He's apologizing to me by acknowledging that my character is significantly more advanced than Sean's, and he doesn't know how he could have forgotten it.

Apology accepted. I squeeze his arm and slip back around the desk to collect my stuff, extra glad now that I cleaned out my locker early. I remember Keisha helping me lug my stuff home and get a little sad again. I'm feeling quiet by the time we get to Andrew's car, and I cover it by checking in with my parents. "School done. H2 A's. HBD,C"—shorthand for "home by dinner or call." I have a group alias that sends to all three of them. If they need me home earlier, someone will say so. But no, I get a thumbs up, a clock, and "11pm" from Mom. I swear, I'm the only one who still uses letters and words instead of hieroglyphs.

"Hi from my mom," I say. "I'm good till eleven."

"Cool. Hi to Mom," Andrew says. And then we just kind of all linger in our own heads, all the way to Andrew's driveway.

I don't go to Andrew's house all that often. Usually we go out, or he comes to mine, because he's the one with the car. When we play SR4, we usually do it up in my room, or remotely on weeknights. I'm glad I brought my laptop to school. It's a treat to play sitting next to each other, instead of across the internet.

It's a small house, just for Andrew and his mom, but the garage has been turned into a den. Well, den and storage room. But still, it's got a carpet and a mini fridge and a TV. It's where Andrew practices cello and goes on SR4 raids, and all that. His room is a no-screen zone, except for his phone. Studying and sleeping happen upstairs. Computer and television and hanging out with his girlfriend and writing papers—that all happens down here.

My room is my world. It's weird to think of a bedroom as just for sleeping and quiet time, instead of as a studio apartment where you do most of your living. The divide works for him. It also means he doesn't have to fight with his mom for the TV in the living room, because it's probably pretty rare for them to want to watch the same things. She needs the closed captions on, and he says they ruin the surprise of what people are about to say. I kind of like the captions for movies, but I agree with him for comedy and other stuff where timing is important.

The three of us flop onto the worn-out leather couch, and Andrew drags over two tray tables for us to put our laptops on before flopping in the cozy space between us. For a second I wonder if he's trying to keep Sean and me apart, like a strategic thing, but then I realize we both gravitated toward the sofa arms and the middle was what was left.

We plug in and boot up. I rest my head on Andrew's shoulder while I wait for my laptop to do its slow warm-up dance. He lifts his arm from between us and drapes it around me, pulling me in closer. When he offers out his other hand, Sean takes it. "How are you guys doing?" he asks quietly.

"Keeping busy is good," Sean says.

"Yeah. That," I agree.

Andrew squeezes and then lets go, getting on to the important business of logging into the game.

We've run the mission three times and the boss guy still hasn't given up the epic blaster. It's random, it's just frustrating that you have to go through the whole thing in order to find out if you've wasted your time or not. Somewhere in there, Andrew's mom comes home and checks in on us. Andrew's unerringly polite, as always. He actually pauses us in a safe little alcove of the space station we're raiding so that he can get up and give her a hug.

His mom, who wants us to call her Shelley instead of Mrs. Novak, but will also answer to "Mom," lost her hearing when her caravan hit an explosive in Afghanistan. Now she works at the school board's main office, in the payroll department. I guess angry teachers are nothing compared to actual bombs, and it's not like she has to listen to them yelling. The next week will be extra busy for her, I imagine. In the meantime, she's just home to shower and change before the end of year office party. She'll be out late, she says, and she's left us some cash if we want to order out for dinner.

We're so immersed that I barely hear the door close when she leaves. It's only the car starting outside the garage door that clues me in, and even that just sounds like a big tremor through the space station at first. Three runs later, we have the blaster, and a ton of extra cash and items to sell. I get up and stretch while the boys take care of that stuff—I'll deal with selling off my loot another time. I text the parents to confirm that I'm staying for food, then go into the house to take a bathroom break.

When I return, I'm startled to hear Keisha's voice. It sounds like it's coming from the bottom of a tin can, but even so, it gives me an adrenaline surge like crazy. Headrush, hands tingling, the whole thing. "Is that the California girl?" I ask, loud enough for whoever's phone is on speaker to pick me up. And I trip over the edge of the rug because suddenly I'm shaking too hard to control my limbs.

The phone is mine, and they answered for me while I was in the bathroom.

"We've stopped somewhere in Indiana for the night," Ki says. "Seriously, you guys. You think the whole country is built up like the east coast, but there's still a whole lot of nothing out here in the middle."

We banter about nothing in particular for a while, and then her parents tell her it's time to get off the phone. Saying goodbye is extra hard for all of us, but she promises to call tomorrow and that makes it a little easier.

"Okay. I'll hang up first," Ki says. "One… two…"

When we've done this before, she always disconnects after two. I'm surprised to not hear the beep of the call ending. That's how hard this is for her. "Less-than-three," I say, and touch the little red phone icon, disconnecting us. Less than three, <3, is a sideways heart.

The mood is dampened now. Not in a bad way, but in a sad, wistful, longing way. We all miss her, and now we're all thinking about her.

"Usually I'd chew you out for peeking at my phone, but thanks for picking up," I say. I rest my head on Andrew's shoulder and he hugs me close to his side.

Sean reaches past Andrew's back to ruffle my hair. "We recognized her ring tone." I have to smile, because the ring tone I've set for Keisha always makes me smile. It's a female singer warming up with an arpeggio—up to the octave and then back down, la la la LA la la la.

I try to snake my arm behind Andrew, but that doesn't work when his arm is behind me, so I reach for Sean past Andrew's chest, turning inward. Soon we're in a weird three-person hug, which should be awkward but turns out to be oddly comforting instead. Andrew kisses me, which I feel a little fluttery about, like it's not fair to kiss in front of Sean when he doesn't have anyone to kiss, but then Andrew turns his head and kisses Sean, too.

Now I'm fluttery in a different kind of way. That's not something I was expecting. Especially not the casual, comfortable way that tells me this isn't the first time. No, this is something sweet and special, and they're both putting a lot of trust in me, kissing in front of me like this without knowing how I'll react.

I reach for Sean at the same time that he reaches for me. Our laptops are still on, still playing the hold screen music for the game, all in sync. I imagine that we're doing what our characters would do to blow off steam after a successful battle. All that extra energy with nowhere else to go, funneled into the celebration of life and flesh and vitality; honoring a lost companion by making sure we appreciate that we still live and feel.

Thinking about this sudden, passionate making-out that way makes it less weird. I've never done much more than make out with Andrew, sometimes with some clothed grinding of hips that I sometimes get off from. Still, the key word is *clothed*. We've always been clothed.

But, I decide, maybe today is the day that we don't stay clothed. Not completely, anyway. We make out, the three of us, in all combinations and with rising hunger, and in between kisses I draw my shirt off over my head. The two of them kiss my breasts, squeezing them, and I unhook my bra when I can't take the teasing of indirect touch anymore.

I need to feel skin on my skin. They're both shirtless too, pale Andrew and dark Sean. Hands and lips are everywhere, theirs and mine, and it's all equal. All one.

I straddle Andrew's lap and rub myself against him. He winces and reaches down between us to readjust himself in his jeans. I can feel him throbbing against me through layers of clothes. I don't want to hurt him, and from the grimace on his face, it's not comfortable for him like this. I open his fly, unzipping him, and stand to push my own jeans down to my ankles. All I'm thinking about is seams and metal zippers and easing discomfort, because apparently I'm pragmatic that way even when my brain has shut off its higher functions. I almost surprise myself to realize that we're grinding in our underwear now, his hardness pushing against me in a way that's so perfect that I don't want to stop. Ever.

It never occurred to me that penises would be warm, like, body heat warm, though there's no reason why they shouldn't be. They *are* part of a body, after all. Still, it's kind of amazing, feeling the way that warmth presses me, fitting along my curve every bit as well as the palm of Keisha's hand does when her fingers are inside me.

Thinking about *that* is what pushes me over the edge. Not the four hands that are on my hips, on my butt, on my chest, squeezing tenderly, even when I want them to be squeezing harder. The tingling through my nethers increases until I think I can't stand it anymore, but I still can't stop. And then I'm breathless and too sensitive for more, and my muscles are spasming and I'm realizing how I've soaked Andrew's underwear. And then I manage a look at his face, and at our laps, and I realize the wetness isn't just mine. He's climaxed too, all up his chest and my stomach, sticky and slippery and cooling quickly in the air where our bodies have parted.

"That was hot," Sean whispers, caressing both of us.

"That was *so* hot," I agree.

There's not buckets and buckets of ejaculate, like in the porn I've seen online. I dip my fingers into it and find a weird texture, like a really thin gel. I'm not sure how to wipe my hand off gracefully, so I lace my fingers with his, hoping it'll rub off onto him. He's done this before. No doubt, he knows how to clean it up better than I do.

I look back up and meet Andrew's intense gaze. I can't seem to look away, but if he's trying to communicate something to me with his expression, it's in a language I don't know. For all his innuendo and big talk, he's never made a real move on me before. He might just be overwhelmed. I know I am.

Sean slides one hand into my hair and one hand into Andrew's. One at a time he kisses us. Deep, long kisses full of tongue and desire. I think I have a second dance left in me, and I'm suddenly hungry to learn what he feels like, too.

I ease off of Andrew's lap and stretch out on the rug, on my back. I extend my arms, inviting Sean to join me, and find that he's already on the same page. Underwear straining, he prowls on top of me, crawling all the way up my body, and settles against me. He doesn't care that I'm sticky and sweaty. He fits himself to me, lips to lips and core to core, and his hips press and grind in a magical way that leaves me breathless.

Andrew slides off the couch and sits beside us, petting us both while we pant and moan. It doesn't take long before I'm over the edge again, ambushed by sensation, and then in that spent place where I can't take any more. Sean's right behind, tensing up on me, his heat spreading across my skin.

After, Sean takes a few moments to catch his breath, raising up on one elbow and looking down at me. After a moment's thought, he brushes my hair out of my eyes.

"I like you," he whispers. It sends a shiver through me.

"I might like you a little, too," I answer. I roll my hips and it makes him gasp, which makes me happy.

"Wanna be my girlfriend?" he asks.

I turn to Andrew, who's gazing at us both with eyes that are glazed and sated. "Mm-hmm," I say. "If my boyfriend doesn't mind."

My boyfriend reaches out, tilts my chin, and lets his lips speak emphatic approval.

We drop Sean off first, and then Andrew takes me home. I'm feeling like I want to cling to him and never let go, but I also need some time alone, to think. My brain is full, my heart is full, and I don't think I've ever craved a shower this badly in my life. No one would care if he came in with me for a little while, since I'm home well before curfew, but I don't offer. It's been a long, emotional day and he still has to turn around and drive back home.

We kiss, and hug tightly, and neither of us says much. Something's deepened, and it's comforting to see him look as solemn as I feel. For tonight, that's enough.

"Tomorrow?" he asks. Saturday night is still our date night.

"Wouldn't miss it." Reluctantly, on shaky legs, I get out. It takes me two tries to close the car door properly, which shows how flustered I am. I call hello and get an answer back, but I manage to get in the house and up the stairs without anyone seeing the rumpled state I'm in. It isn't until I'm up in my room and kicking off my shoes that I realize I never did eat anything for dinner. Or lunch. And that my shirt is inside out.

I nudge the door shut behind me and drop my stuff beside it. I'm so grateful to have my own bathroom. I smell weird, like sweat mixed with school paste, and when I strip off my shirt, it sticks to me in the front and pulls away stiff. I start the water before I take off my jeans, then survey them, too. They seem unscathed enough to go in the regular laundry, but my shirt and my underwear are coming into the shower with me. My bra is… Hm. I don't know where my bra is. If it isn't in my backpack, it's still in Andrew's couch cushions somewhere. That's an awkward conversation I can put off till tomorrow.

My underwear are white satin with black swirls all over them. I test the water with my hand, and when it's hot enough I step into the shower with my panties still on, and holding my shirt. What was wet when things were exciting has now dried into flakes that turn sticky again when water hits them. You never see this part in porn, and I never really thought about where a guy's semen goes after the act is over. I figured it all goes into the condom, or it gets… I don't know. Evaporated or something.

It's not gross, but it's definitely strange to me. Also, I can't see it being mistaken for anything else. We mostly wash our own clothes around here, but if they run light sometimes the parents will throw mine in, too. The last thing I need is for someone to get suspicious over my laundry.

I use a lot of soap on my shirt and on myself. By the time I'm rinsing and wringing out the clothes and hanging them on the towel bar inside the shower, it looks like all the evidence of my evening is gone.

I use the hairdryer to clear the condensation from the mirror, wrap my robe around me, and stare at my reflection for a long time. I feel different, but I look the same. I wonder if what we did tonight counts as sex. That's the biggest question I have right now, the one churning over and over.

The one I just can't figure out how to answer. Technically, penetration is sex, and there wasn't any of that. But there were orgasms, and that's sex. What Keisha and I do counts as sex, beyond a doubt, and there are no penises involved anywhere in that. There's nudity with Ki, though, and there wasn't nudity tonight. Not technically. I didn't see their bits. Nobody touched anything directly with bare hands. Still, there was intensity, there was pleasure, and there was definitely release.

Am I technically still a virgin? I've been having sex with Keisha for a while now, intense enough sex that neither of us has a hymen. I think sex with a girl totally counts, but I also think first times with a girl and with a boy are different things, so was this my boy virginity or was this just "messing around"?

I enjoyed it and I don't regret it, so why does it matter so much to me what I call it? It's not like I'm going to tell anyone about it.

Then I realize why it matters so much, or at least a small part of why: I'm rehearsing in my head for what I tell Keisha. How do I tell her that we did this without her, immediately after talking to her? Would she be jealous, or touched, or mad, or… ? Her moods have been so unpredictable lately, it's probably not safe to mention it at all.

And does she know our boyfriends are—I recall the word my dad used—"cozy"? There's a chance that she does, and that I'm the last to know. But I also recall what happened when Andrew thought he was the last to know that Keisha was moving, and how that almost sent everything nuclear. If she doesn't know, it's not my place to out them. Not even to her.

My stomach growls, as if in agreement.

"Right?" I ask it, and immediately feel silly. It growls again, this time with a hollow ache, and I remember Priority Two. I still need to eat something.

I change into leggings and a long shirt, tie my hair back, and head downstairs. Somewhere down there, cheese, crackers, and my normal, recognizable life are calling to me.

CHAPTER 9

THE parents are all watching a cheesy sci-fi movie. Rather, they're all messing around on their phones and tablets in the living room, while the movie plays on the television. I join them, snagging a corner of Mom's blanket.

"Cold toes," she says, and traps my feet between her calves to warm them. I feel like I've come downstairs wearing a Halloween mask or something and nobody's noticed yet, but it's only a matter of time before they realize something is different.

"Long day," I answer. "Ki's family left this morning."

Mom squeezes my feet. "How are you holding out?"

"Okay." I search for something else to say. Falling back on the truth always works. "I helped out in the library all day, and then we killed a lot of pixel aliens at Andrew's house."

"What did you have for dinner?"

Oh, right. That's where I was going when I came down here. "His mom told us to order pizza but we got too wrapped up in things." It's like Ozone can sense that I'm about to get up, because he hops right up onto my lap and sprawls out. His giant floofy belly is exposed for petting. Unlike with most cats, it's not even a trap. I sigh and splay my fingers through his fur. "That's okay, cat. I wasn't hungry anyway."

I fall asleep on the couch, under the cat. When I wake up, the television is off, the lights are out, and the blanket has been spread over me. Ozone is on top of it, perched on my hip like a purring, shedding paperweight. Everything is dark and still, so it's probably well after midnight. There's a policy in our house that unless it's specifically requested of you, you don't wake someone up to tell them to go to sleep. Usually I appreciate that, but my neck complains when I turn my head. Then the cat complains when I try to sit up.

"Everybody's a critic," I tell him. Even tickling his ear with his tail doesn't get him to move, and he usually hates that. I end up wrapping him in the blanket like a burrito and moving the whole assembly off me, onto the cushion. He stays like that, still purring, watching me like I've just abandoned him on some stranger's doorstep. I'm used to his betrayal-face, so I don't let him guilt me into carrying him upstairs.

I grab a couple slices of cheese from the fridge and nibble them on the way up to my room. Half aware, I rummage for my phone. The battery's completely drained, so it just flashes a red empty rectangle to chastise me when I plug it in and start the power flowing. That empty rectangle represents me pretty well at the moment, I think as I get under the covers.

My bed feels big and lonely, and I feel out of sorts. It's Friday night and Keisha isn't here. She hasn't even been gone twenty-four whole hours yet, but her absence has already changed everything.

Ozone serenades me awake, singing me the song of his people. There's a particular hunting cry he only makes when he's carrying his fabric carrot toy around and wants acknowledgment for it. I'm not sure if it's a "praise me" cry or a "help! What do I do with it now?" plea. I just know he wants the attention.

The room is brighter than I'm used to it being in the morning, which is good because it means I've slept late. After finals and everything, I needed it.

I throw on a black tank top and a flower-print long skirt, pick up my phone, and take the mirror selfie I promised Keisha. I don't have any messages from either of the boys. It's not that I was expecting anything specific, but some kind of sweet, romantic message, after what happened last night, would have been… well, sweet and romantic.

They were probably as tired as I was. Everything is undoubtedly fine.

I wonder if either of them have messaged with Keisha. It's pointless to let myself think any further down that path without knowing. Too many what-ifs to get myself worked up about for no reason, when my brain is already too willing to get anxious over nothing. They're not going to say anything for the same reason I'm not going to say anything: none of us want to hurt her, and she'd be hurt if we made her feel like she's missing out.

Mom is in the kitchen, talking on the phone in animated Spanish, while Brenna sits at the table cradling her coffee and watching with vague amusement. Mom is either talking to her parents or Dad's—not just because they're the only people she speaks Spanish with, but because she's talking about lots of mundane, domestic stuff that would be boring to anyone else. It's all how I'm working in the library for the summer and they're thinking of getting the tile replaced in one of the bathrooms. I sneak around her to pour myself some coffee, and she snags me in a hug before she lets me go on my way. I'm not fully awake, but I've got my order of operations set: Hug. Coffee. Banana. Bagel. Chair.

By the time I settle in next to Brenna, Mom is passing along congratulations to someone whose dog has just had a litter. Brenna's name and mine pop out at us amidst the rapid fire of conversation.

"What did we do?" Brenna asks me under her breath.

"Nothing. Don't worry, we're just an alibi," I whisper back.

Brenna's knowledge of Spanish isn't non-existent, but it's about on the level of what you'd learn in high school. She can piece things together if they're written, or if someone's talking at a teaching pace, but when it's the fast patter of native speakers, she's happy to glaze over and let one of us translate.

I stir a bunch of sugar into my coffee, test it, and add a little more milk. Brenna asks me for the latest news on Keisha, and I tell her about the phone call last night. That's the most current news I have.

"What's Andrew doing for the summer?" she asks.

I know he's told me, but it takes me a few seconds to remember. "College prep course, at the library. A lot of people in our class are taking it. It's like summer school for practicing standardized tests."

"Didn't you already take your SATs?"

"Yeah, we took them this spring. But they're offered again in the fall if you want to up your score, so…"

"So Andrew wasn't happy with his score?"

"He wants to go pre-law. I don't think he'll be happy with anything less than perfect."

"What's less than perfect?" Mom asks, bringing her mug over and leaving the phone on the counter.

"Andrew's SAT scores," I answer. "But not by much. Who was on the phone?"

"Your aunt Marisol," she says. "Sorry for giving you allergies, but she was wearing down my resolve. I had to do something drastic or we'd have ended up with a house full of dogs."

"It's okay. I don't think I'd want a house full of dogs. Will they be okay, though?" I curl my hands around my mug. It's still too hot to drink, but it feels soothing.

"They'll be fine. I think she's secretly hoping everyone turns her down so that she can keep them. She'll probably get your grandparents to take one or two, though, so remember to sneeze a lot next time we visit Abi and Belo."

Dad pokes his head around the door frame. I hadn't heard him come down the stairs. "Allie? Can I see you a minute?"

Normally I'd respond to something like that with a dad joke: "Ta-da. See?" But there's a solemn look on his face and it frightens me a little. Frightens is maybe a little strong. It sobers me. It's not the in-trouble look, exactly, but it's serious and he doesn't want to talk in front of my other parents.

"Um… sure?" I exchange glances with Brenna and Mom but they don't seem to know either. It isn't until I'm climbing the stairs, following him to my own door, that I realize I've still got my coffee mug in a death grip in both hands. My stomach is actively trying to burrow out through my feet.

What did he find in my room?

Mentally, I retrace my steps from last night. Or maybe I'm seeing my adolescence flash before my eyes. I don't have contraband. I don't sneak drinks or anything. I don't think I even have any leftover Easter candy up here. I'm squeaky clean, except for the clothes hanging in my shower… which are also clean.

Dad gestures me in ahead of him and follows with a sigh. "Sometimes I wish you were still little and I could still protect you from the world," he starts. Not an auspicious beginning. But he doesn't close the door, so even if it's private, it's not super secret. That's worth pinning hope to.

I sit at the desk—it seems more equalizing than sitting on the bed, which would feel all kinds of vulnerable. There's a crisp sheet of paper on my desk that I don't see until he rests his fingertips on it, tapping lightly.

It's not the clothes in the shower. Is it grades? I'm an A/B student and finals went well. It can't be grades. I don't know what to say, so I wait.

"I hate to make you start your vacation with stress, is all." He turns over the page. Words and numbers, and what looks like an email header. "They installed the new gravestone. We had an estimate before, but this is the final bill. It's a lot, but if you work hard this summer…"

I'm not used to looking at numbers as big as the grand total at the bottom, but once the shock of it fades, I'm okay. This is the least bad of all the bad things it could be. The actual isn't that much more than the estimate, except that I hadn't expected that we'd be charged for removal of the old stone and re-landscaping and all the other incidentals. I thought I was just paying for the new stone. I can hardly protest, though, when Dad's paid for the car and will keep paying for it—insurance policies get more expensive once you've had to actually use them.

"I have some saved already." I remember to breathe. "I've been working on it."

He nods and rests his hand on my shoulder. "I know. And I know the timing is bad. It came in last night, and there was no way I was going to hit you with it then, when Keisha's just moved. And I didn't want to make it a big thing around the table, you know? I don't want you to feel like you're on trial. But you want to be grown up and responsible… this is what it looks like. Bad news when you don't want it. Also, we'll need to go visit the family and formally apologize."

And oh, he doesn't say, but I already know it, *is that going to suck.*

I lean in and he hugs me. At least grown-ups still get hugs.

It's my first time in the car since we've gotten it back. The big dent in the front is gone, like it was never there at all. The new airbag is hiding in its little compartment. The car has that new car smell, I guess from living at a repair shop for a couple weeks.

Dad drives and I'm not the navigator. The GPS has taken my job, and I feel like a useless extra person who has no reason to be in the car. I'm not even the ensign. I'm like the cargo. I tell this to my dad.

"You're the ambassador," he argues. "The diplomat. You bring apology and overtures of peace."

I glance at the potted lily I'm holding in my lap. Even it wants to wilt away. But Dad's trying and I appreciate that, so I try, too. "We come in peace for all mankind," I venture. A sidelong glance shows me that he's nodding, with a smirk. Those are the words humans left on a plaque on the moon. It's going to take more than an apology and a stupid plant to make up for this, but that's what the money from my summer job is for.

All I know about the family is that their last name is Wendell, and the deceased were Arthur and Grace. It's hard to tell anything about them from names like that. Arthur and

Grace sound like a winning ballroom dancing team. We're visiting their son, Bradley Wendell, who has a wife and two kids. I don't know any of their names.

I follow my dad up to the front door, holding the plant with both hands instead of holding the skirt of my sundress down against the breeze. I'm glad I've got cycling shorts underneath it. The universe won't embarrass me this time.

The door opens and it's Paisley, from the library. She's wearing a peach-colored tank top with a cute matching short-sleeved cardigan over it, both of which look like they've been ironed. I'm so surprised to see her, that's all I can focus on for a minute. She rolls her eyes, then turns and shouts for her dad.

"I guess come in?" she says, like she's asking us more than telling us. Then her father is there in the doorway, shaking Dad's hand and then taking the plant from me, inviting us into the perfect front parlor living room that, obviously, no one ever uses except for serious company. It's that kind of house, one for having everything in its place, not one for living in.

Mr. Wendell returns without the plant. Paisley and I are still stealing looks at each other. After that first eye-roll, her expression has turned blank. I can't get a feel for what she thinks about her late grandparents, or anything else.

The rest of the family comes in. Mrs. Wendell gets introduced to Dad as April, and they shake hands. The college-aged guy is Paisley's older brother Cecil.

"Family names," April assures Dad warmly, with one hand on each of her kids' shoulders like they just happen to always be posed for portraits anytime they're in the same room. It's a kind of formality within a family that I've never known, and it feels weird. Cecil's barely older than me and he's wearing slacks and a polo shirt with a collar, just for lounging around the house? It's beyond weird. It's an alternate universe.

Nobody else starts, so I guess it's up to me.

"So," I say, and all the eyes turn toward me. I don't know where to look, or who I'm supposed to address. I wipe my palms on my skirt, even though they're not sweaty. "As you obviously know, I accidentally hit your family's tombstone with our car. I'm still learning and it went out of control. We're here so I can apologize. I'm really sorry, it's my fault, and I plan to work all summer to pay for the repairs."

I can't tell if that breaks the tension or ratchets it up. For a moment nobody says anything. Then Cecil moves. He takes a framed photo from on top of a piano that I hadn't even noticed, and brings it over to me, gesturing for me to sit on the sofa. Everybody else, by some unspoken sign, sits too. He's beside me, and I should be thinking about anything in the world except how he smells, but he smells fresh and clean and *male*, the way Andrew smells clean and male, and last night comes back to me in a rush. I can't help thinking that I'd like to burrow in against Cecil's neck, with my lips at the place at his nape where he's got peach fuzz. I'd just nibble and breathe.

But he's got a photo in his hands, and he's saying words. "This is Grandma Grace and Grandpa Arthur."

I take the photo from him gently and cradle it in my hands. It's black and white, starting to fade, and has a crease in it but not between them. She's wearing a white dress and a fantastic big hat, and he's got a suit and a pocket watch on a chain. They look older than my parents but younger than my grandparents. In their fifties, maybe?

"Did you know them?" I ask. I'm asking Cecil, I assume, since he's the one talking to me, but I feel stupid the moment the question is out of my mouth. No, I shouldn't feel stupid. I'm asking about them. I'm expressing interest in the family.

I'm making it personal. All things Brenna said when I asked her for advice. Focus on their life, not their death, and definitely not the fact that I basically desecrated their grave.

"A little," Cecil answers. "Grandma made clothing by hand. She made all our baby clothes. Grandpa carved figurines, and he made all Grandma's buttons that she used."

"That's really sweet," I say, stroking fingers along the edge of the frame before sitting back and making distance. "Thank you for sharing that with me."

The room is tense. Whatever the right response was, that wasn't it.

"Would you like to know more about them?" April asks. "You could both stay for lunch."

If I made a list of the things I least wanted to do in the whole world, staying for three courses of heaping guilt would definitely be there. But, I did the thing and this is my punishment, and at least Dad is here with me. He gives the faintest nod of encouragement, so I smile as warmly as I can, and lay it on thick: "I'd love to. Daddy, can we?"

I survive lunch, and come away from it feeling... less guilty and maybe more forgiven. Also, quite stuffed. I might have zoned out a little on the finer points of emigrating from Europe in the early twentieth century, but Cecil kept fidgeting and touching my foot with his foot under the table. I don't think it meant anything, considering what I was there for, but it added to how jumbled up I am about last night. He took a friendly interest, though, so at least one person in that family didn't hate me. That's how I'm looking at it.

Well, three people. The parents seemed impressed that I was so interested in making amends to them and to their deceased loved ones, as if a desire to learn about them was enough of an apology to erase all fault.

Paisley didn't do more than shoot odd glances in my direction, but neither of us mentioned that we knew each other.

I dress up a little extra for my date with Andrew. We may not be doing anything more than sitting in my room and watching movies, but I feel like looking nice for someone I *actually* like. He shows up in slacks and a button up shirt with a collar, so I feel like I've made the right call. He comes in and says hi to my parents, makes small talk, the whole thing. Then he asks if I'm ready to go. I don't know where we're going, but I trust him, so I say yes and get my shoes. When we get into the car he leans over and kisses me, gentle and sweet. I fight the urge to bury my fingers in his hair.

There's a lake not far from where I live. It's a little man-made thing, nothing particularly notable or special. It's non-notable enough that I tend to forget it's there, but I recognize that we're heading toward it. It's busy tonight, with a makeshift overflow parking area on the grass that's already half full. A bored guy who looks familiar—from my history class, I think?—guides us to a parking spot.

There's some unloading of supplies from the trunk: a cooler, a well-laundered school board tote bag with a blanket stuffed into it. I take the blanket from him and we follow the crowd down to the wide field beside the pond. At the far end, a screen is set up.

"Picnic and a movie?" I ask.

He nods, giving me a sheepish grin. "If it's not too trite."

"It's the best. Really."

We find a spot and I pull out the blanket. Nestled at the bottom of the bag: insect repellent lotion. Now the best date is even better.

The movie is a classic film noir mystery I've never seen before. Most of the audience is older, but I see some couples and groups that are closer to our age, too. It's like a drive-in without the privacy, but that's a good thing. With privacy, after last night, I'm not sure what would happen, and I'm not sure I'm ready for what my body would probably tell me it wants. It's practically all I've been thinking about, but it's good—it's a relief, almost—to not have it as an option.

The spread is good, too. Berries, vegetables and dip, cold meat and cheese with crackers. Chocolate. Each little container is a new surprise. We don't talk through the movie, but we nibble, we kiss a little, and eventually we pack up the empty containers and curl up together.

Counting the drive-in, this is only the second time I've ever been to a movie where the lights don't come back up after the credits roll, but it's the first time I've had fireflies as wandering ushers. Our way back isn't a challenge as long as we step carefully. We don't even need to pull up the flashlight apps on our phones.

I stop at a bench where the grass meets the concrete path, tugging him over with a light squeeze of his hand. We sit and watch the procession of other movie-goers returning to their cars. I have too many things queued up to say, all things I've been thinking about all day, and all of them are fighting to go first. As a result, there's a bottleneck and I can't get any of them to come out. I reach for something I can shake loose, something easy:

"I think my bra might still be in your couch."

Really, brain? That's what we're leading with?

Brains are jerks.

"It's up in my room, actually. I found it when I got home last night, and I…" Andrew's not one to get flustered, but he looks down at our joined hands and smiles sheepishly. "I might have put it under my pillow. You know, for safe keeping."

Brains may be jerks, but hearts are idiots; when he says that, mine melts. "Wow. How did that work out? Did the breast fairy visit you during the night?"

Our voices are low, but his laughter isn't. A few people turn to glance our way at the sound. He ducks and fits his smiling lips right to my ear. "I love your breasts, by the way."

I shiver, and not from the touch of his breath. When he pulls back, I want him to come back and make me shiver again.

I want to ask him if he's a virgin, but I don't know if that's the word when it's a boy's first time. I want to ask him if he's talked to Keisha. I want to ask him how long he's been making out with Sean, but in a way that sounds supportive and not weird. I don't know how to make words for any of those things.

"Are you getting cold?" he asks me. "Would this be easier someplace else?"

I shake my head. "If we're alone, it'll be too tempting to do things that aren't talk."

He nods, and that smile flickers back across his lips again. "Okay. I don't know when they'll kick us out, but I'm good here till then."

"Was that the first time you… ?" I let it trail off because I'm not sure what to ask. I'll play it safe and let him answer it the way he hears it.

He shakes his head. "I've messed around before. Not exactly like that, but… you know. 'Everything but.'"

"With a girl? Or a boy?" It comes out archly instead of as neutral curiosity. My cheeks feel hot.

"Oh. Yeah. I don't know what that was, with Sean, but it felt good and I just went with it. I don't know what it means.

I don't know if it has to mean anything." He shrugs. "I'm not in love with him, but I'd do it again. That's the best I've got right now."

That's a good summation. I rub my cheek on his shoulder. "Have you talked with him about it?"

He shakes his head again, rubbing his chin across my hair. "I hate that guys aren't supposed to talk about our feelings. It's like, it's a sign of weakness to admit that things matter to you. Girls are supposed to talk about feelings, so you can kind of trust a girl to start it off. But, if there's no girl in the equation, who does that part? Maybe we should, but we don't."

"I remember my first real date with Keisha. We got to the restaurant door and kind of both expected the other to slip ahead and open it. It was only a second, but I know. Stupid gender roles."

"So, who did open it?"

"She held the first door for me, and then I held the second door for her. We take turns. Just like I do with you. Whoever gets there first. But that wasn't instinctive. It was a thing I had to stop and double-take about."

His sigh is soft, but can I feel it in my hair. "Yeah. Yeah… I hear you. It's just weird. I never thought about that. Who holds the door, I mean. But yeah."

CHAPTER 10

T HE library has conference and meeting rooms upstairs. I hardly ever go up there because my job is on the main floor, but the big, classroom-sized meeting room is where the test prep course is being held. It starts an hour earlier than my shift does, so it gives me a little tingly jolt to see Andrew's blue Prius in the parking lot when I get there.

Inside, everything's basically normal. I haven't worked opening shift since winter break. The energy is different first thing in the morning, sleepy but full of potential. I put my phone in my pocket and stow the rest of my things in the locking cabinet under the main info desk. Janice is running off a list of holds on the computer. She nods good morning to me, but she doesn't talk more than absolutely necessary when we're out on the library floor.

Janice doesn't wear glasses or put her graying blonde hair in a bun, but she takes the silence part of the librarian stereotype more seriously than she needs to. She scolds the volunteers if they sharpen the pencils too loudly. Apparently, according to Janice Gregory, pencils should be seen and not heard.

If that's true for pencils, it's doubly true for teenagers. When the class upstairs takes a break, at least two dozen people stream into the library, while a handful more head outside. Andrew makes a beeline to me and I scoot around the desk for a silent hug and the quietest possible kiss. Sean is right there, his arms waiting, when Andrew lets me go. I hadn't even known he was taking the course too. I give him an equal hug.

I want to hang out, but I need to get back to work. I apologize, they say no problem, and I go back to checking in books. But it's not like I can concentrate when they're off together, talking quietly enough that I can't hear them, knowing they're glancing over at me now and then. I check the same book in three times. Then break is over and they're being summoned back upstairs. Both boys peck me little kisses. They walk out together, so close their arms almost brush.

Janice is frowning. She's not frowning *at* me, but still. Even though I'm all tingly from their attention, I know I'm going to have to manage myself better going forward.

I contrive to take my afternoon break when the class lets out, so that I can go out to the picnic table and hang out with the boys, without disturbing the patrons. It's right about when the parents are bringing their little kids in for story time, and I exchange waves with the people I recognize from Sundays. I go back inside a couple minutes early to help get stuff ready. Paisley sidles up next to me as we arrange miniature chairs into a rainbow of arced rows.

"Hey… Is it true you're dating both those guys?" she whispers to me.

I blink, stop, and then have to rush to catch up to her. It's not the question itself that perplexes me, it's the other part of what she's just said. "What do you mean, 'Is it true?'"

She shrugs and doesn't make eye contact. "So, is it?"

"Well, yeah. Kind of."

She nods knowingly, says, "I *told* Cecil, but he didn't believe me," and leaves me to finish the chairs. Out of curiosity, I follow her through the stacks. Ostensibly, I'm going around picking up stray books from tables, and it makes me miss Keisha and her little tableaux. I wander past Paisley and one of the other volunteers whispering together toward the end of an aisle, hunched over something on a phone screen. They both straighten and go quiet when they see me, with odd strained looks on their faces. Paisley is smiling too hard. I've got a sinking feeling that if I'd heard what they were saying, I wouldn't be happy. The rest of the day, that's a feeling I can't shake.

I slip back around to the children's section. I'm not completely naïve, but I'm so used to multiple partners as a thing that it takes me most of the day before I suddenly wonder if she was messaging about my answer.

Coming up with an explanation doesn't stop me from thinking about it. The weird question and the rush to go send a message. It's not like I'm going to lie and say I don't care about people when I do. I'm just not used to anyone caring who I date. I'm sure I'm blowing it all out of proportion. Nobody cared when I was dating Keisha and Andrew at the same time, after all. Even if nobody really knew, that was also just because they didn't care. Maybe they still don't "care," they're just bored. But, still. It wasn't on anyone's radar. *I* wasn't on anyone's radar. And apparently, now I am.

After dinner, I get a text.

"Hello from the highway. Breaking news: girls are so rude," Keisha messages, and there's a screenshot of a text window. When I enlarge it, I see that Paisley has tracked Ki down on Facebook to tell her that her boyfriend is already running around on her with her BFF. Ki follows the picture with: "Duh, right?"

I'm not sure how to translate "Duh, right?" in this context. Is it "of course you're all hanging out" or "of course I know you're messing around"? Because the implication is that of course we—the four of us—communicate, so it's not like anyone could tattle on any one of us to any other of us. It's not like anyone could tell Keisha anything she doesn't know, because we don't hide anything from her... except that I don't know if Keisha *does* know. And it's not like I can ask her if she knows.

I send back: "Shit-stirring is so 7th grade." That seems safe.

Ki returns an emoji of a hand waving. We've dubbed that the *hair-flip*, between us. It means "whatever," as in "this person/thing is not worth our time."

"We all miss you like whoa," I add. "This is cheesy, but: it's brought us closer." It's an understatement, but it's not a lie.

"Consoling each other, I hear?" So she does know, at least to some extent. She follows it with a winking face, so I send back something playfully naughty about holes that only she can fill. That's also true; nothing we did went past the surface. I wait for her playful response. And wait.

And wait.

"Everything okay?" Brenna asks from across the table. It must be showing on my face.

"Keisha must have gone out of signal range. It's nothing." I pull up Sean's name to message him, but then stop with the text box still blank. What am I going to say? *Did you tell our girlfriend we messed around? Because someone did.* What if he didn't? Then it'll sound accusing and he'll get upset. Or maybe she's just trying to be cute and has no actual idea at all.

A couple days later I'm shelving books, fairly absorbed in the work, when somebody raps on my book cart like they're knocking on a door. I jump, heart pounding, and turn to see Cecil, Paisley's brother.

"Oh, hey," I say, trying to sound casual. What I want to say is that startling people isn't very nice, but I'm kind of in debt to him and his family, so I keep that to the inside voice. "Are you looking for Paisley?" I ask instead.

"No," he says. "I'm looking for you." He drapes his arm across the back of my cart in too familiar a way, like he thinks everything exists for his convenience.

"Oh. Well, you found me. Filed under—" I take a quick glance at the nearest shelf, "under Mysteries." Inwardly, I cringe at myself.

He smiles, showing me perfect teeth. "Nice. Want to go get a coffee?"

A dozen thoughts race around in my head, bumping into each other and tangling into knots. "Um, sure?"

"Great." He stands back a pace, slipping his hands into the pockets of his slacks. *Slacks.* It's not even a school uniform or anything. He just casually wears slacks.

I pick up the next book, weighing it. He doesn't move.

It takes me a minute to realize that he's waiting.

"Um… did you mean now?" I ask.

"Sure," he says, echoing me. "Why not?"

"Cecil, I'm kind of working. I know Paisley's a volunteer and everything, but this is my job and I'm on a shift. I can't just pick up and go."

"Oh," he says, like it hadn't occurred to him.

"Why does she volunteer here, anyway?" It seems like a safe enough question, and I want to put attention somewhere other than on me.

"Yeah. Our mom's on the Library Board and Paisley's got to do community stuff for her college application, so...here she is. I figured you were a volunteer too. So, tomorrow, then? I can pick you up here at closing time, and take you home after?"

He's still kind of cute, and he smells nice, I'll give him that, but he exudes so much confidence that I want to shake him up just to see what it looks like when he falters. Honestly, it's almost the only reason I say yes. The other reason being that it got him out of my face. He doesn't look like he's used to people saying no to him, and that means that a no might just intrigue him more. I'm not saying yes because it will annoy his sister, though of course I know it will. It's not even to gain insight into their bizarre family—I already know that's what I'll be telling people later. It's to shake up his tidy little expectations of what girls are and what they want.

"Okay. Tomorrow is good."

"Good." He squeezes my shoulder on his way past me, and then I'm alone with the books again.

"I ran over his grandparents and he asked me out. I can't help thinking it's a trap. Or a prank." I'm on my bed, lying on my back with my feet propped up on the wall and my phone against my ear.

"The hot rich guy asks the library girl out on a dare, or to set her up so his hot friends can have a laugh?" Keisha adds. "Straight out of a chick movie."

"Yeah, but what kind? The romcom kind or the horror kind?"

"Hmm. That *is* how they got Carrie to the prom…"

It's too ridiculous to worry, so I have to laugh. "No danger there. He's not taking me to prom. You are."

She laughs too. "Sweet-talker. So, what are you going to wear?"

I haven't thought about that yet. "Um, clothes? Like, a skirt and a nice top?"

"Bzzt," she says. "Wrong answer. He's expecting you to make an effort to impress him, so don't. Wear jeans. And if he tells you how 'real' you are and how 'refreshing' it is, you owe me a cupcake."

I blow her a raspberry. "You're on. So, what's up on your end? Tell me about drama camp."

"It's not too dramatic. If this is what college drama class is like, I'm in for a long, painful ride. Today we had trust and body exercises and variations on charades and stuff. That's the warm-up. Then there was an improv thing where we were in pairs and groups. Then more movement, like modern dance almost. And then lunch and a lecture. The teacher wants us to call her Mare, short for Meredith, I think. She wears ballet clothes to class. She's always telling us to be more in touch with ourselves."

"What about your fellow thespians?"

"I don't know yet. There's nobody I hate from day one, so at least that's something, right?"

"Totally. It's just started. Give yourself time!" I tease.

"Ha. Right. Oh—and we'll be having guest instructors. 'Real Hollywood actors,' but she won't tell us who. Like, it could be seriously famous movie stars, or it could be some guy who was an extra in an allergy pill commercial."

"He aspires to move up to be the guy who gets to sneeze?" I say, and we both giggle.

I know better than to call her out for being happy, because that'll just get her self-aware and shut her down, but I'm buoyed by how engaged she sounds.

"Tomorrow's assignment is a selfie in date clothes," she says. "And there had better be jeans."

"Yes, ma'am. And yours is a video tour of your new apartment. I know it's probably all boxes, but I don't care."

She mmms under her breath, a content little noise. "How'd your parents react?" she asks, as an afterthought.

"Yeah. That's kind of next on the agenda."

She stifles her laugh into something that sounds like a snerk. "Your dad. I can't wait to hear what your dad says."

"Yeah," I say, a little sourly. "Can't wait."

"Well, describe it to me in detail, okay? Including the look on his face."

"Hey, don't you have more drama club people to tell me about? One by one?"

"Oh, no, missy. You have a date with hilarity. I'd be a bad girlfriend if I got in the way of that."

I sigh. "Too transparent, huh?"

"Maybe. Go on, be brave. I'll still be here after."

"Promise?"

"Always."

My stomach is fluttering into my throat and I don't know why. I don't know what I'm afraid my parents will say, or think, or… whatever. This is probably a bigger screwed-up thing to me than it is to anyone else, except maybe Paisley. But I don't even know her, so why should that matter? I only know that she volunteers in the library even though she goes to a private prep school, not to Central with us.

It's weird how nervous I am, but it's also weird how much Keisha telling me to do this has bolstered me. I'm so used to following her lead, I guess. I go to the bathroom—not stalling!—and consider taking one of my low-dose anxiety pills. No, it'll take half an hour to kick in, and waiting that long *would* be stalling.

"Why am I so nervous about this?" is the mantra I whisper in my head all the way down the stairs, toward the growing scents of dinner. The tile floor at the bottom is a shock to my bare feet, and I realize suddenly that I could just play it off as "I'll be home late, I'm getting a ride," and they wouldn't think to ask if it was anyone other than Andrew.

That's definitely an option. The more I think about it, the better it sounds.

There's stew with noodles in the slow cooker and crusty bread on the cutting board on the counter. Ozone is pacing and whining, but he won't jump up on the table—at least, not while people are in the room. He rubs on my legs when I make myself a plate, but when I take a seat at the table he moves on to pester someone else.

"How was work?" Dad asks. I shrug.

"So," I say, "it turns out Paisley Wendell, whose dead grandparents I ran over, is volunteering at the library this summer, and her mom is on the Board." No need to mention that she's been there all spring and I sort of know her already.

"Small world, huh?" Dad says.

Mom, ladling herself some dinner and pointedly ignoring the cat, adds, "Well. *That's* not awkward."

"For real," I agree. "I think she was texting about me to her friends or something."

"Did you text *your* friends?" Brenna asks.

"Of course I did. And I told my whole family at dinner,

too… but I waited until after work." There's something deeply satisfying about having better manners than a rich girl who practically lives in a Perfect Homes magazine, but I don't add that part out loud.

Dad chuckles a little and Brenna looks proud. Mom looks like she's trying not to elbow Dad in the side for laughing.

"Oh, and speaking of work, I'm going out after, tomorrow, if that's okay. I'll be home by dinner."

They all look at each other and no one objects. This half truth, non-forthcoming thing is pretty easy, and it only comes with a fraction of the guilt of an actual lie. Sean would probably call it a life-hack. But really, I seriously doubt Cecil has told his family that he's going out with *me*, so that makes it fair.

Totally fair.

Keisha seems less convinced about the total fairness, but she's glad I'm being honest with her. I tell Andrew, too. "Have you had a real date with Sean yet?" he asks me.

Honestly, I haven't thought about Sean as a separate entity, and it takes Andrew's question to make me realize it. He's part of the group, and that's comfortable and good, but aside from how he seems to know a back way or an inside guy or whatever, in everything he does, there's nothing I really know about him.

I should fix that, I acknowledge, but not right now. After I get through tomorrow.

CHAPTER 11

TAKE my morning mirror selfie, in a green wraparound shirt and black jeans. My curls are unruly, so I pull them back in a headband. The shirt has a v-neck and it looks bare to me, so I put on the necklace Abi and Belo got me for my Quinceañera—a gold heart with tiny diamond chips around it. It's small and subtle, but it hangs at just the right spot.

Paisley is out today, so at least that's one slice of awkward I won't have to face. I imagine coming out after work to get into Cecil's car, and getting into a stalemate with her at the passenger side door. Yeah, no.

I seek Sean out when the class goes on break, and we sit at a picnic table, lightly touching hands and talking about nothing important. It's awkward, but in a flirty, fun kind of way.

"So hey, I've been meaning to ask you," he breaks in, with sudden intention. My heart thumps.

"Okay… ?"

"Why does Andrew always knock *and* ring when he's at the door?"

Of all the things I'd have expected to be asked, that one didn't even make the list.

"Isn't that a question for Andrew?" I ask.

He shrugs and flashes me his disarming grin. "Asking him would be awkward, right? Drawing attention to something weird?"

I'm not feeling flirted with anymore, and immediately I find I'm not feeling flirty anymore, myself. Instead I'm feeling like I'm still on the info desk. *Oh, boyfriend info? That's under human relationships. Try Social Interactions, around 302 on the shelf.* His charming grin, I realize, is a tool, not a reaction.

"When his mom lost her hearing, they got an accessible doorbell. People would knock on the door instead of ringing, even though the bell was right there. He'd tell her someone was at the door, but she didn't like having to rely on him for it. It's not a weird thing, it's a really aware thing. You never know what's going on with someone when you come to their door."

Sean sits back. "Wow. I wouldn't have thought of that. I knew she had hearing aids, and he signs at her, but…" He shrugs. "He doesn't make a thing of it."

It's one of Andrew's most admirable qualities, I think. He quietly does the right thing and doesn't ask for a gold star for it. It's an example I try to follow.

Thinking that brings along a pang at the mild deceit of my parents. Well, I didn't say I was perfect at it. Besides, not bothering them over a trivial one-time thing *is* the considerate option.

I glance at my phone. Break time is almost over. "What about you?" I ask. "You don't talk about home-stuff. What's your story?"

He gives me the grin again. "It's complicated."

I laugh. "Yeah. Look who you're saying that to. Try me."

He bows his head, conceding the point. "So, Mom and Dad split up. Which is to say, Dad splits. Mom remarries, they have a kid. Mom dies—breast cancer. Stepdad remarries. They legally adopt me. So I live with my step parents, more or less."

"Oh. Wow."

He shrugs. "It might as well be foster care. It's not like they're my real parents. It's just a waiting game at this point. Once I'm eighteen, I'm out of there."

Does Andrew know this? Does Keisha? Losing your parents must suck. I can't even imagine.

I draw breath to say so, and to ask, but he pats my hand. "Time to go."

I head back in with him, but not quite *with* him. Everything feels off, like the ground is a little farther away than usual. We're walking close but not touching, and it's like we're not quite in the same world together. Like maybe we never have been, but I've never noticed it before.

Andrew is at one of the front tables, reviewing study guides, and looks up when we come in. "And?" he signs to me, a subtle movement like the start of a stretch. I make a face that answers "meh," and wander close enough to give his hand a warm squeeze before I head back to work.

I'm not the one Sean is interested in. Andrew is, and Keisha is, and that's cool with me. I got caught up in the moment—and it was a fun moment—but I don't have to date *all* the people, and there are ways to be close that don't involve kissing. I wonder if Sean's realized yet that I'm not an entity to him, either.

Cecil doesn't come inside today. That's good. Maybe he's gotten the message that this is work for me. But I keep expecting him to turn up over my shoulder, so it's not like I'm able to focus. I almost start to think he's a no-show, but once I step out into the first hint of evening breeze, I see him lounging on the nearest bench.

I'm still smarting a little from my chat with Sean, so when Cecil asks if he can hug me, I say yes. His shirt is a crisp white button-down, but he's gone casual, neatly rolling up the sleeves.

Cecil's hair is almost as light and fine as Andrew's, though his eyes are darker. He's got an intensity to him that I'd put down to age, or confidence, that was comforting when I was floundering out of my depth at his house. Now, on my turf, it seems misplaced. Aimless, almost.

"Hi," I say, stepping back. "How's it going?"

"Well!" he answers with a big smile. "So, coffee?"

"Sure. There's Three Beans just up the street, or Penny's further down."

"Which do you like better?" he asks, his smile making a sly twist.

There's no parking at Three Beans, and it's just a couple of blocks. I'm not sure I'm comfortable strolling down the street together. And the staff there all know me.

"Penny's has really good Mexican hot chocolate," I answer.

He draws his keychain out of his pocket. "Will you navigate for me?"

"Sure." Navigating reminds me of riding with my dad, which reminds me of the accident. I reflexively rub the back of my neck. "Which—oh," I trail off with a little laugh. There's only one car left in visitor parking. The fancy silver one.

He leads me toward it. I'm not much of a car person, but I know that the curvier and smoother a car is, the bigger a deal it is. This thing could be a flying saucer. Even the door handles are recessed flush until he does something—or the car detects his brainwaves, maybe, when we get close enough—and the chrome rectangle slides out ready for use.

Cecil looks at me like he expects me to make a fuss over its awesomeness, so I don't. I do let him get the door for me, and I thank him once I'm tucked up inside. It's a quick trip, but it's long enough for me to appreciate the inside of the flying saucer and the purr of its electric engine.

Penny's is in an older brick building that used to be a townhouse. The upstairs entrance leads to a café with a long pastry counter and little two-person tables with dainty curled-iron chairs. There's a staircase inside that connects to the lower floor, which has couches and a stage for live music, and serves wine. The coolest thing about Penny's is the floor—living up to its name, it's tiled with a mosaic of copper one-cent coins, varnished over. Ditto, the tables and countertops.

Cecil grins a little, breaking his own sophisticated varnish to show a little childlike wonder at the intricate designs made of bright and dull coins. Our table has a Greek braid sort of border, and when he traces it with his fingertip it occurs to me that this is the first thing he's done that's made him seem human to me.

I order the hot chocolate, and he does too. Then we both sit back and there's that moment of silence that always marks the beginning of any desire to chat.

"How do you like library work?" he asks. As ice breakers go, it gets an A. Taking interest in what interests the other person, asking them about themselves, not about someone else.

"I like it a lot. I'm planning to go into Information Science in college."

"Really?" He sits forward. "That's great, being so clear on what you want to do. What do you love about it?"

"Classification systems," I say. The waiter comes with our drinks in oversized polished copper mugs, with whipped cream and a thin cookie on the saucer. "I'm fascinated by how we mentally put things in boxes to bring order to the world, and even make different sets of boxes to order the exact same things. I might have taught myself the Dewey Decimals by heart," I add, as if it's an afterthought.

His eyes crinkle mid-sip, and his mouth mirrors their smile when he lowers his cup. "You know most colleges use That Other System, right?" I laugh because I can hear the capital letters in how he says it.

"Library of Congress is a valid lifestyle choice," I answer, and he laughs happily because I got his quip.

"Where are you applying?"

"That's… an interesting question. Is it weird that I haven't thought about it much? I guess I just figured I'd go wherever Keisha is going."

"Keisha?"

"My girlfriend. She's studying drama, and she doesn't want to go to a school named after a problematic old white guy. That kinda limits the local options, you know."

"Yeah, it seriously does. There's University of Virginia, that's named after a virgin… but it's got its own problematic old white guy associations. University of Maryland? Also named after…"

"The same virgin," I agree. "But if she went to Maryland and I went to an old dead guy school, like GW, maybe, or Georgetown, we wouldn't be that far." It's the first time I've said this out loud. It feels disloyal to the plan, but it was always Keisha's plan, not "our" plan, and I don't think I'd stopped to think about that aspect of it since she moved and everything else. It's been so easy to just follow her lead, but now she's not here and I am.

"The Metro is good for that. I can get here from GW anytime. Hey, you okay?" Cecil asks, reaching partway across the penny table as if he can touch my attention itself.

"Oh." I'm sure I'm blushing. "Just falling down the admissions-anxiety rabbit hole. Sorry!"

"My fault," he says, ducking his head. "It's so nice to talk to a girl about something other than college, and then I default to 'so…college?' It spoils you for human conversation, college does. Now you know."

"Cool. So, now that orientation's out of the way…"

"Right." He smirks. "Because Paisley says you're dating guys, and you just said you have a girlfriend."

"Ha. Well played. Yeah, I'm equal-opportunity." It's out before I realize how it will sound, and I drop my face into my hands right as he starts to laugh. "Not…"

"I mean," he says, bringing his napkin up to the corner of his eye. "I know what you mean, but… admissions. That can go so many ways."

I groan. "Affirmative action. Yikes."

He touches my forearms with his fingertips, the look on his face saying that he's suddenly aware of being a white guy talking to a browner girl. "I didn't–"

"No," I lift my head and touch his fingers. "It's okay. I know." I don't know why I'm reassuring a guy I'm not even interested in that I'm interested in guys, but at least I know he gets that I'm trying to say I'm bi. Not that I'm open for applicants. When I drop my hand away, he retrieves his. There's no spark to the touch; no flirt in it.

"Well, how about you, since we're sharing?" I say.

"You're not assuming I'm straight?"

"The majority of people in my life aren't." I shrug more casually than I feel. But it's true. Not even my parents are straight. "So it's not a thing I automatically assume."

"Fair enough."

"But, if that's too personal, it's okay to say so. What's your major?"

We both make each other think, and I appreciate that. When we finish, the sky is fully dark and a jazz guitar has started up downstairs. Cecil reaches for the check, and I make a noise in protest.

"You're saving your pennies," he reminds me, rapping his knuckles on the coin table for emphasis. It startles me into remembering that he's not just a random interesting guy I'm having coffee with. Once I feel the jolt of remembering that, I wonder how I possibly could have forgotten it, even for a moment.

"You can pay when we get coffee to celebrate paying off the new headstone," he offers, and I back down.

"Okay. Just not at the actual site, please."

"Deal."

It's a short drive to my neighborhood. I navigate and he follows my directions with ease. "Oh," he says when we pull up to my house, "you live across the street from Loudon Quinn." That's not a thing I was expecting him to say.

"How do you know Loudon?" I ask.

"She hangs out with Paisley. I've been the taxi service once or twice."

"Huh," I say. "Small world, right?"

He smiles. He hasn't shut the car off, or even shifted it into park, and I'm glad. This is just a drop-off, not a chat. "Thanks for hanging out with me," he says.

"Thanks for coffee. And for, you know, humanizing this whole weird thing."

"Anytime. Hey, I'll see you around."

I get out, wave, and start up my front walk. Like Andrew, he doesn't drive away until I've opened the front door.

The next morning, Mick, who's in the prep class, looks me up and down, and then makes a rude gesture with his tongue against the inside of his cheek when he passes me.

Hair-flip icon, I decide, and try to let it roll off me. But the class is on break, and I don't see Andrew or Sean among them. They must have stayed upstairs. I'm disappointed, but it's just as well. I don't want another stern look from Janice.

We have a staff safety drill once the class goes back upstairs. This consists of a video we watch every month that tells us what the code words are that signal different kinds of danger, and what to do if we can't get to someone to use a code word. It's a result of growing up in the age of school shootings, I guess, and "if you see something, say something." It's mandatory for public libraries. Code Blue means active shooter. Code Purple, Code Orange, Code Red… they all mean different things. There's a poster back in the office, too, in case there's any chance we might forget. But some of the volunteers are new and it's their first time, so for their sake I try to look like I'm paying serious attention, even though really I'm just wondering what Paisley is up to and why Andrew and Sean didn't even come downstairs with the rest of the class.

I try to keep busy. Shelve books, pick up books. There's not much of either to do. It's summer break, after all. No one's doing research, and the retired folks who come in to trade one stack of mysteries or romances for a new stack don't usually leave extra books lying around. A few people wander in to use the computers. Mostly it's just slow.

Slow gives Paisley a lot of time to smirk at me, and gives me a lot of time to notice. Janice knows something weird is going on between us, so she's watching us more carefully. Which doesn't help. She knows the difference between real work and busy work, and she doesn't let me hide in the stacks making sure the DVDs are in alphabetical order if there's actual stuff that needs to be done.

Then I realize that if I stay where Janice can see me, Paisley can't be as obvious. Suddenly, it's like Janice is my new best friend. Well, no, I'm not *that* blatant, but I stop trying to wander off and hide.

"So, you and Keisha keep in touch?" I imagine saying, but there wouldn't be any point. She knew that if she stirred stuff with Ki, it would get back to me. The only way to win is to show her that her bullshit didn't affect us at all. And the only way to do that is to bring it up in a context that makes it sad that Paisley doesn't have better things to do. I'm not good at manipulating people, and I'm kind of glad it's a skill I've never had to develop, so I'm content to leave that game to more skilled players. You can't get clobbered if you refuse to take the field. Or something.

When class lets out, I watch for the boys. They're stony-faced and sullen when they emerge. Andrew's gaze sneaks toward me, but he doesn't give anything away even when our eyes meet. He's not usually this guarded, so if I didn't already see that he's on edge, I'd know it now.

He makes an *L* with the fingers of one hand and touches it to his other open palm, like he's pantomiming a clock. That's ASL for "later." He means we'll talk later and he'll tell me what's going on. That comforts me a little, and if a little is all I can get, then a little is enough.

Janice clears her throat. I've been staring out past the door, I guess. Whoops. I get busy checking in books and trying not to meet her gaze.

Even though the prep class has very little to do with us while they're here, somehow it feels a lot emptier just knowing they've gone. Lonelier.

I take a bathroom break and text Keisha. I don't have any more to say than I did last night, but after reaching out to her and seeing her morning selfie, I feel a little better. Then it's back to the grind. Paisley's grandparents' gravestone isn't going to pay for itself.

"Is this what having a real job is like?" I ask my parents over dinner. "Just the same thing every day: standing around and trying to look busier than you really are?"

Brenna laughs, while Mom and Dad exchange a look.

"Pretty much," Dad says. "Even desk jobs are like that sometimes."

"Like working in a store when there are no customers and you've already run out of things you can do to look like you're doing something?"

"Just like that," Dad agrees, "except that you're also surrounded by things that would pass the time but that aren't work, and you can't get caught using any of them on company time."

"So," I start, pulling my frustration into words, "why does society put so much importance on everybody having a job, when so many jobs are practically just people standing around and waiting for the workday to end?"

"Good question," Dad says. "Think about that while you're at work tomorrow."

I make a face at him, and he laughs.

Another thing I wonder is whether it's later yet. As in "I'll tell you about it later." After dinner I send Andrew a message and ask him to call.

He comes over instead. We haven't had face to face alone time in a while. Even our last date was in the middle of the park, so we weren't actually alone.

He knocks, then rings the bell.

We're heading into summer, so it's still light out after dinner. Twilight has just started to settle over the neighborhood and there's a cool, gentle breeze shooing away the worst of the day's heat. I don't want to go back inside, but I don't want to go anywhere either, so I compromise and ask him if the back deck is okay. It's private, but it's not "mess around" private.

We sit close on the loveseat. He puts his arms around me and I curl toward him for a long, comforting hug. We don't kiss, not yet. He tucks my head under his chin and rests his cheek on my hair. We stay like that a while, quiet and still, just breathing and holding hands and being close. After the last few days, an oasis of calm silence is nice.

But it can't last forever. "So," he starts quietly, "today was interesting."

"Yeah?"

He shakes his head. "It's nothing. It's just kids being kids. You know?"

"Being kids *how*?"

He chews on his lip. I wait. Tangled up with him is a comfortable place to be. I'm content to wait.

"Some of the other kids are confused by our relationship."

"Why do they care, and how is it any of their business?"

"Everything people do is their business, especially if it's stuff they can have opinions on."

"They *can't* have opinions. Their opinions don't matter. Just don't pay attention and they'll stop."

He laughs. He *laughs* at me. "Have you ever seen that work?"

I think about it. I haven't.

I sigh. "One of the girls asked me about us and tattled to Keisha, trying to get her mad. It didn't work." I don't explain about the small-worldness of the girl being Paisley.

He bites his lip again, then gives in. "One of the guys suggested a theory that Ki moved away because Sean and I are boning and she asked her parents if they could move, in order to get her away from here."

I stare at him till I realize I'm staring. Then I settle back in against him. "That might be the dumbest thing I've ever heard."

He shrugs. "I'm not disagreeing. I'm just saying, this is the shit that's being stirred. They don't get why this is okay; why me and Sean aren't competing with each other like you're up for grabs. And if there are grabs for them, too."

That explains the lewd tongue thing. They think I'm up for auction and they're pissed that they haven't been invited to bid… even though they've never cared that I was alive before. I guess that's what happens when someone has something that you don't. You want it too, just because. "So, what do we do?"

"Nothing, really. They're not threatening us or doing anything illegal. Just, you know, we can't rise to it."

"A minute ago, I could swear I heard you say that ignoring it wouldn't make it go away."

"It won't. But now I'm not talking about making it go away, I'm talking about keeping our noses clean. We stoop to retort on their level and we'll be the bad guys. We protest, they say they hit a nerve with us so they must be right."

That makes sense to me. Not that I like it, but it makes sense. "But that means they get to say whatever they want, and we don't get to say it's not true." I lean my cheek on his shoulder. His shirt is cool and smooth against my skin.

"C'mon," he says. "Don't let them ruin it."

I'm not letting anyone "ruin" anything. How can you retroactively ruin something that's already happened? Andrew takes my stony silence as something it isn't. He tightens his arm around me.

"Are you mad?" he asks.

Few things make me as mad as someone asking if I'm mad.

"Yeah, a little, but not at you. I don't like being this week's news cycle. Why does it suddenly matter now when it never mattered before?" I know the answer, I'm just venting.

"You weren't dating two boys before."

Yeah. That.

Three, if my date with Cecil is also making the rounds. My point, about why it's anyone's business, still remains. And there's another matter, too. "I'm feeling like messing around with Sean was a one-time thing. We got caught up in the moment and it was fun, but I don't think I want to date him."

Andrew holds me in silence while he thinks about that. "Your chat didn't go well?"

"Not really. We're…better in a group, I think."

"Hm. What do you want to do about that?"

I make a face, even though he can't see it. I'd like to do nothing about it, and have a situation resolve itself for once. But that's not going to happen. "I owe it to him to give it a try, I think. One date won't kill me. Maybe it was just bad timing, or something."

"Maybe," he agrees.

"Have you talked to Keisha?" I ask.

"About our gaming night? No. Have you?"

I shake my head against him. "Not really. Has Sean?"

"I don't think so. We should really coordinate," he says.

"What, like get our story straight? There's nothing to get straight if we tell the truth."

"Yeah," says Mister Future Pre-Law, "but what's the truth?"

CHAPTER 12

ANDREW does some prodding, I think, because Sean messages me, setting up a date. It doesn't sit right with me, but I'm not sure if it's because I'm hypersensitive and looking for warning signs, or if the things I'm uncomfortable about are real.

Brenna says she has a minute between clients, so I run down and tap on her door.

"Hey," she says, opening the door and inviting me into her waiting room. She's wearing makeup and is dressed all business-serious. "What's up?"

"Can I run something by you?"

She nods. "Of course."

I take a deep breath to put my words together. "I have a date at the mall, and I don't know how I'm going to feel about taking a Metro train home alone that late."

"Can't Andrew drop you off?"

I can feel my cheeks reddening and I can't stop them from doing it, even though going out with someone who isn't Andrew isn't a thing I need to be ashamed of. Not in this

145

house. "I won't be with Andrew. I'm hanging out with Sean, Keisha's boy."

"And he's not seeing you home?"

"Probably not. We're meeting there, so…" I shrug.

She frowns a little, but recovers quickly. Then she thinks about it and frowns again, for real. "You don't have to do anything you expect yourself to be uncomfortable with. You know that, right?"

"It's complicated," I say, because it is. I don't tell her how hard it was for us to agree on something to do together; I don't tell her that I get exhausted just thinking about reopening that conversation to come up with a Plan B. "I'm not uncomfortable with seeing him."

"You're already anxious about how you're going to get home from seeing him—which is fully justified, by the way. I'm not comfortable with you taking Metro home alone at night, and your parents wouldn't be either."

"Is that an official veto?" I ask.

"I think so, yes. Only because you're uncomfortable. I mean, of course I'd pick you up, but the bigger issue is you feeling like you have to compromise your comfort and safety for his convenience. Reschedule and make plans that you feel safer with, and feel free to blame it on me."

She's right. I shouldn't compromise the basics for anyone else. He should have offered to see me home safely, at least. I didn't want to ask him to because that would leave him walking back to the subway alone when it's even later. But she's right. That should have been a flaw in the plan, not something I brushed off just to make a plan happen.

She hugs me, one-armed, and then ruffles my curls. "Let me know what you end up doing instead."

I nod and hop back upstairs to my bedroom—and my

phone. I have an awkward conversation ahead of me, and I'd rather be awkward by text than by voice. At least typing gives me a little more time to plan out what to say.

I have a message waiting from Keisha. It's a photo of a thick, beaten-up paperback of "theatre monologues for girls" with a rainbow of tape flags marking the pages. "Pick a color," she says in the next message after the photo.

"Infrared," I send back, just to be a brat. She sends me a smile and a heart. I feel like I've done something right.

That bolsters me a little, and I pull up Sean's contact screen. "Hey. So, change of plans. I'm not allowed to take the subway home that late. Did you want to come over instead?"

Sean comes over, but it's not comfortable like when Andrew comes over. "What do you want to do?" he asks, lingering in the foyer after I hug him at the door.

"We could watch a movie," I say, but his face falls, so I continue, "or play video games." The frown doesn't move. "Or go for a walk… ? Are you thirsty?"

Nothing. He shrugs, hands in his pockets.

I recall a few conversations with Keisha that felt like this, before she moved away, where it felt like I was doing all the work and she wasn't even trying to help keep it going.

One more try: "Well, what did you and Ki usually do when you hung out?"

He shrugs again, but this time it's one of those shy shrugs that means "I don't want to come out and say we didn't do anything but mess around, but…"

Sigh. *Really?*

I never asked her how far she'd gone with Sean, or any boy, because it wasn't a competition between us and the answer wouldn't have changed anything. It occurs to me suddenly that in those last few days when she was extra amorous with me, it was because they'd gone all the way. I'm not sure how I feel about that. For now, I wait him out. I want to make him actually say it.

This is so awkward. If I had psychic powers, I'd use them to make some kind of distraction. Girl Scouts at the door. Ozone pushing a mug off the counter. Anything to make this moment end.

"Ki's just… she's really forward, right?" he says finally. "She knows what she wants to do and you go along with her and it's fun."

Is he saying I'm less fun than Keisha, or is he saying that I'm being too considerate and he doesn't actually want to have a vote in what we do? How am I supposed to decide for him if he frowns at everything I suggest? Am I supposed to just keep trying things until I hit on an option that doesn't make him frown, or is he telling me he *wants* me to steamroll over his opinions?

Or is he justifying the fact that they mostly just messed around by implying that it was her idea and he was somehow helpless and blameless?

Meanwhile, we're still standing in the entryway, he's got his back to the door, and I'm at the point where I just want to go up to my room and read. By myself.

"So?" he says, like it's my fault we haven't made a decision yet. Maybe he's forgotten that I'm the one who's been doing all the suggesting.

There's nothing to be gained from being indirect, so I just take a deep breath and ask it: "So, when I asked you over, did that sound like 'I just want to make out and stuff' to you?"

"Well, yeah."

I exhale. I realize I was hoping for any other answer. I don't want to make out with him. "I'm really sorry. I didn't mean to give you that impression."

"You'd said it was okay, though," he points out. He's leaning back against the door now, blocking it. He probably doesn't realize he's blocking it, but it makes me feel threatened and a little claustrophobic. If he gets mad, I don't know how I can make him leave.

"Not… I mean, not making out and stuff. I didn't say that was okay. I did say it would be okay to go out tonight, but then I ran it past Brenna and she said it wasn't."

He doesn't react when I address my consent or my expectations, but when I finish his brow furrows. Out of what I've just said, what he's latched on to is his relationship to authority.

I know what he's going to say before he says it. And I know that once he says it, we'll be done. Big-time done. "But she's not your parent. What did your parents say?"

And there it is.

He sees it in the look on my face. I'm not angry, I'm just disappointed. "It's not like she gave birth to you," he argues.

"Neither did my dad," I answer. I gesture to the door behind him. "Maybe tonight's not so good after all. I'm sorry for making you come all the way out here on mixed messages."

"So you're not… ?"

"No. I think it's best if we don't."

He doesn't hug me again. He doesn't say much of anything. He barely gives me a wave before he closes the door behind him.

I cross to the stairs and sit heavily on the bottom step, staring at the front door. "What the hell just happened?"

I don't realize I've said it aloud until I hear an answer.

Mom comes around the corner from the kitchen. "You stood up for yourself."

My face fits neatly into my palms. "How much did you hear?"

"Enough." She sits down next to me, hip-checking me to scoot me over an inch. "It feels crappy, but no matter how crappy it feels, not standing up for yourself always feels worse."

I sigh.

"I'm sorry," she says. She doesn't put her arm around me or pat me or do anything patronizing. I realize I'm braced for it, and when it doesn't come I relax a little.

"How is this so easy for you?" I ask her. "All of you."

"It isn't. We made a lot of our mistakes when you were too young to notice them. When things come up, we try to handle them behind the scenes."

"So you just make it *look* easy?"

"Pretty much. You screw up and then you pick yourself up and deal with it. Welcome to being an adult." She bumps my shoulder lightly with hers.

I bump back. "Great. Thanks."

"You know what else is part of being an adult?"

I lift my head up a little. This is where I expect something not adult-like at all, like "adults can have ice cream for dinner"—something to placate me or distract me. "What's that?"

"Owning yourself. You decide when someone gets to kiss you and when they don't. If they don't accept it, they're not worth you."

I'm impressed, and kind of touched. Big points for Mom, for going the adult route after all. Twice, even.

We sit in silence for a few minutes. I stare at the door, replaying Sean's whole visit—what there was of it—in my head. I don't know what Mom's doing, besides waiting.

I line up what she just said with what Brenna said earlier. It makes me think of these placemats we had when I was a kid. They were clear plastic with a geometric design on them, and when you stacked them all, the designs would combine into a bigger image. It's like that. Sticking up for my comfort stacks with the right to get to decide who gets to touch me, and with the fact that one "yes" doesn't mean it's yes every time. I get that… but I'm not sure the stack is complete yet. There's at least one big piece of the design that's still missing: how to stand up for my choices when other people are hurt by them, or just don't understand them.

Keisha likes Sean. Andrew likes Sean. I like the person Sean is when he's around Keisha or Andrew. Without someone else's lead to follow, he's just not…

I don't know how to finish that sentence. Then I think maybe it's complete already.

He's just… not.

I could share what I'm thinking. I could ask how it works when you don't see the same things in someone that other people do, and how you explain your feelings without insulting their choice, or making them feel like they have to win you over to their viewpoint.

Mom probably has a ready answer, but I can't make myself ask, no matter how many ways I try phrasing it in my head.

Maybe part of being an adult is figuring these things out for myself.

I buff my cheek on Mom's shoulder like a cat, and pull myself up by the railing.

Up in my room, I look at my phone and my laptop screen. On the computer, a string of nonsense characters trails four lines deep in the active chat window. I press enter on it. Apparently, Ozone wanted to say hi to Keisha, too.

When she writes back an hour or so later, she says, "Hi, purr-monster." It makes me smile.

"Which monologue did you go with?" I send.

"Ingenue choosing which boy to date," she answers. "So stupid. Date them both!"

She wants me to laugh, so I do. In text, anyway. In reality, I squirm a little. *What if she doesn't actually end up liking them both?*

"Speaking of, how's things with our boys? Aren't you supposed to be out with S?"

So he'd told her that much, but not that things went stupid. Interesting. I pick my words carefully: "We couldn't agree on what to do. Decided to call it a night." I think about explaining more, or defending him, but I leave it simple.

"Don't be too mad at him. Test prep kids are assholes and he's taking it hard."

That, we could have talked about. "That sucks," I answer. "Wish he'd told me. How bad is it?"

"He didn't say. Gotta be all 'I can handle it,' right?"

"Sigh at boys. I miss you." I type it, delete it, and then type it again. I don't want to cling, but it's not being clingy if it's true.

"Miss you too, chica. It's not forever. We'll be college roommates before you know it."

I sit back and sigh. What college, though? That's another conversation I don't want to have.

Instead, I take a capture of the screen. It's the thought that counts, and that's what I should stay focused on. I might just print it out and hang it on my wall.

It's Saturday so there's no SAT class, but I still have to work. Every time I think about ducking out of it, I remember the big stupid tombstone I have to replace before I can learn to drive for real. I shower and dress, and photograph my outfit for Ki—it's part of the routine now—and get to the library just before ten o'clock.

Dee Kurtz is behind the desk today. She's Janice's boss, and it's unusual to see her out on the floor. I say hi and stow my stuff, and log in on one of the staff computers to print out the hold list.

"Alicía, may I have a moment?" Dee says.

A chill passes through me. What now?

I follow my grandboss into the back. She's tall and she always wears matching polyester pants and blouses, with orthopedic support shoes. Her hair is short and poofy, and it's that straw color you get when you try to dye blonde over gray. Her shoes squeak a little on the linoleum. When my shoes squeak, I always try to change how I'm walking, to see if I can make them stop. Not her. She owns the squeak, or maybe just doesn't notice. There's a rumor she lives with a woman, and that they're romantic partners.

"We've had some complaints about your behavior. That it's inappropriate in front of children," she says.

I hugged Andrew and Sean, and I've sat out on the benches with them. There might have been a kiss on the cheek once or twice. That's all. Part of me wants to roll my eyes and tell her people are stupid and maybe if there was more hugging in the world there'd be less stress and anger and shootings in schools. Part of me wants to scream in frustration. I split the difference and just nod. I'm not sure how a nod is halfway between an eyeroll and a scream, but it's best if I just go with it and not go down that road. A nod is the best possible answer.

A nod won't get me fired.

"You've been fraternizing with multiple boys from the SAT course, both on the grounds and out on the floor."

"M-my boyfriend, and his best friend." I hate that I stammer, but I can't take it back. I'm not going to pretend I don't know what she's talking about.

"With *multiple* boys," she repeats. It's more a confirmation than a question.

I feel cornered, but I try not to sound cornered. "I'm not any cozier here than I am in school. We hug and stuff, but nothing inappropriate. But, I understand. I know this is a workplace for me, even if it's school for them. I can save hugging my boyfriend for at home."

I had that chat with Sean out at the picnic tables, where he kind of held my hand. I got into Cecil's car that same day. I squeezed Andrew's shoulder. Hardly crimes.

Dee gives me a long, measured look, her lips wrinkly even though they're pressed thin. She's not enjoying this either. "Consider this an official warning. Because the complaints came from parents, some of whom are Friends of the Library, the children's section is off limits to you until further notice."

I nod again. That's not an offer, it's a threat from the Library Board and she's passing it along as gently as she can. Paisley's been up to her passive-aggressive texting, and she's probably gone to her mom, who is on the board. She's got to know that I need this job to pay *her* stupid family, so why does she have to make it harder for me?

"And if you don't think you'll be able to focus on your work with teenage boys around, you can ask to switch your hours for when the class isn't in session."

The SAT class meets most of the day, so only working when that class isn't here would give me… two or three hours a day, down from eight? I'd never get paid off at that rate.

"Okay. Thank you for the warning. I'll keep my focus on the job."

I want to protest and argue, or at least defend myself, but I don't have the footing to. She could have just fired me, if patrons and donors complained—Friends of the Library is basically a fundraising board, so the administrators take their feedback very seriously—but she didn't. For that, I really am grateful. It would be impossible to get another summer job at this point, now that school's been out a few weeks.

"Oh—here," she says, and hands me an envelope. I take it. "The hold list is probably done printing."

And that's my dismissal. I nod, fidget with the envelope, then turn and head back out to the floor. There's nothing else for me to say. I expect my eyes to start stinging with angry tears, but they don't. I feel curiously empty, flat... it's a little like the numbness I felt after the accident, and I wonder if I'm in shock. Do physical and emotional shock even work the same way? I suppose that would be under Human Physiology. Maybe I'll look it up sometime. It's around 610, maybe 612.

I get to the desk, remember the envelope in my hands, and open it. It's a window envelope, business-sized, with my name and address showing through the clear part, but it's not sealed. I peek at the amount on the paycheck inside and breathe a sigh. It's the full amount it should be. I haven't been docked as punishment or anything. Not that I would have been, but still, considering the way things are going...

When I go to put the check in my bag, I remember what I've forgotten.

My period is regular like clockwork. It always hits right at the end of the month, give or take a few days, so it usually aligns with payday. I left home this morning without supplies.

I rummage in my bag and manage to pull out one stray pad. Its protective outer wrapping is warped but intact. I make a quick trip to the bathroom, relieved to find that it hasn't started yet, so at least that's one thing that hasn't gone wrong yet today. Armored against nature, I'm ready to go pull the books that are destined for the hold shelf.

I get all the holds put back into place. All except the ones in the kids' section, of course. It's pretty quiet. No surprise— it's a summer weekend and the weather is gorgeous. No one's coming here to study, and families are mostly off outdoors or on weekend trips or something. We've got some patrons dropping books off, and a bus from the local senior center bringing folks to trade in their books, but even the computer terminals are mostly vacant.

An easy day *should* pass quickly, but it doesn't. Instead, I have way too much time to think. I wonder all day about which patrons complained. I know I'm just spinning my wheels on it, but knowing that doesn't make the wheels stop. It's like there are little brain hamsters in them, racing to nowhere in my head. My anxiety medicine is in the bathroom cabinet at home, and right now home feels really far away.

CHAPTER 13

ANDREW belongs to a community swimming pool, and he asks me if I'm interested in a swim and movie night thing they're doing tonight. *Killer Flounder From the Deep.* It sounds like a fun time, so I say yes. It's only when I'm home and changing into my swimsuit that I remember my period and how it will literally be starting at any moment.

Naked, I rummage through the drawers in my bathroom for my moon cup. It's a rubbery lavender thing that you use like a tampon, but it holds more blood and you can wash and reuse it. Once I've got that in, I finish changing. Now I feel prepared for the worst. I throw a loose sundress over the swimsuit and pull a clean towel from the closet. I hear Andrew's knock-and-ring just as I'm sliding into my sandals.

Andrew picks me up wearing a long-sleeved Towson State shirt, and board shorts with little fish all over them. He's had way more time in the sun than I have, and it shows in his tan and the cornsilk highlights in his hair.

"You know I hate horror movies, right?" I ask him in the car. He squeezes my knee. "I'm counting on it."

"Because you like subjecting me to things I don't enjoy?" My tone may be playful, but I'm suddenly thinking about my failed date with Sean.

"Because I'm hoping you'll be scared and you'll need to cling to me. Wet bodies pressing together in the dark, hearts racing…" He doesn't have to turn for me to see his grin.

I laugh. When he makes me laugh, it's always like the sun's just come out and melted my worries away. For the rest of the drive, with his hand on my leg and my fingers twined with his, window down and breeze in my hair, work and bullies and everything fades into the background.

The lot isn't full, but there's as good a turnout as there usually is during the day, which is impressive. Andrew gets his towel and two flattened pool floats out of the trunk.

He scans the membership tag on his keychain and ushers me through the turnstile, then scans again for himself.

"So now they'll think you're here twice," I tease him.

He smirks at me. "Wouldn't you like *that*. No, we can have up to three people in here on our account."

It's not quite dark yet, but the pool is already mood-lit. The submerged lights have been covered in blue and red gels, turning the water a strange shade of shifting purple. It's strange because it's clear, I realize, as if any water that color should by definition be murky and have fae creatures gliding around in it.

We put our stuff in a locker, drop our towels and shoes off at a pair of lounge chairs, and he hands me one deflated float. Still deep in thought, I start blowing.

I'm not even trying to tease him, but Andrew gets this fascinating look on his face. It's not his sly innuendo face, it's something much more serious. Like the expression he made when he knew he was going to climax against me but before he was sure he wanted to give in to it. Undisguised lust, maybe? It makes me tingle to see it on him, whatever it is. I think I like it.

I finish and seal the little plastic cap. He clears his throat, shifts in his seat, and holds out the other limp plastic disc. "Will… uh… will you blow mine?" His eyes sparkle mischief.

I hand him the finished one. "I did just blow yours. Was it good for you?"

He actually blushes. Clears his throat again.

I laugh. "Will you blow mine?"

"Oh, no. Please. You do you. I like to watch." I level him a look, and he relents. "I guess reciprocation is important. Isn't that what all the women's magazines say?"

His blush deepens when he lifts the port to his lips. He's squirming under the scrutiny, and breaks off a few times to laugh. I've never seen him so flustered. It's kind of awesome.

His trunks have a pocket with a zipper, because as always men's clothes are practical where women's clothes are just supposed to be pretty. He tucks the locker key in his pocket. All we have at our spot are shoes and towels and cover-up clothes, nothing worth stealing. Not that anyone would, but it's still not worth leaving an open invitation.

"I like this old-movies-outdoors trend we've got going," I tell him, giving his hand a squeeze.

"I like old movies. They're a product of their time, whether they mean to be or not. It's interesting to read between the lines. What was important to them, what they thought the future would be like, that sort of thing."

I know what he means, and I realize I think about it too, even if I don't do it as consciously. Every generation, every culture, has its own ideas of what success looks like, or what the worst thing that could happen would be.

I'm assuming this movie is about staying alive; success probably looks like getting rid of killer fish, or maybe trying to figure out why they're attacking people. Usually in these things the only ways to deal with a threat are to kill it or do something to heal it, fix it, and make it not dangerous. Or sometimes you get the conflict between those two camps. The scientist begging the soldier not to shoot, it's just frightened and hungry and in pain. Or because it's the only one we've ever seen and we need to study it, but that's selfish, not sensitive.

As we get into the water, sitting on our floats so that we're basically reclining with our ankles trailing in front of us, I'm thinking about how this applies to the mess I'm in now. The library is giving me another chance, so they're trying to repair me instead of firing me. Paisley's the ringleader, mad because I hit her grandparents' grave, inciting the other kids to kill us by poisoning our environment. I'm the dumb fish that got swept into the cove by mistake, and I'm just trying to find a way back to the open sea. I'm flopping around, but it's not because I want to hurt anyone or break anything or get in the way. I'm just trying to figure out which way to swim.

Yeah, it doesn't really work at all.

Someone jolts into my tube from behind, startling me and sending me flailing into Andrew's.

"Where's your boyfriend?" It's Mickey, the lewd-tongue guy from prep class.

"He's right here," I say, grabbing for Andrew's float.

"I wasn't asking *you*," he says, turning his expectant gaze on Andrew like he's still waiting for an answer.

The boy has beady eyes that bulge like marbles. He turns them back to me, looking me up and down. The water is warm, but his stare sends a sudden chill through me, and when he ogles my chest I know what he's seeing. My bile rises. I wish I could stop my body from showing that it's cold. I don't want it putting on a show for him to mock. Where's a jerk-eating fish when you need one?

"Oh hey, Mick. My boyfriend? Oh, he took the night off," Andrew says, unflapped. I wait for the reciprocal insult; the "your mom wore him out" or whatever, but Andrew doesn't go there.

Mick is waiting for it, too, but it never comes. Andrew doesn't say anything else, just gives the same expectant look the guy gave him. Unfulfilled, the creep mutters something under his breath and wades off. The girl he goes back to is Paisley's friend, the one she was whispering over her screen with.

"Ass," I say quietly once he's out of range. "How do you keep it together when they do that?"

He shrugs. "They're just trying to get a rise."

"Yeah, I know, but when he's up in my face, my blood pressure doesn't care."

Andrew takes my hand. His is shaking. It's not cold; it's nerves. I meet his eyes, a question in mine.

"My blood pressure doesn't care either, but hell if I'll let *him* know that."

Andrew is going to make a really great lawyer.

Killer Flounder From the Deep, as you'd figure, really wants to be a horror movie. In general, it fails spectacularly because of its weak plot, its horrible script, and its laughably dated special effects.

But, watching it in the water goes a long way toward bringing the scary back. As predicted, there are scientists who want to study the fish and angry people who want to kill the fish, and stupid people who keep getting in the water with the fish. Everybody shouts at the screen when people get into the water, as if enough volume on our part will break some barrier and let us warn them. People really get into it. It's kind of awesome.

There's a definite unease through the crowd, and everyone is much more into it than they would have been without the water lapping at their arms and legs. I'll have to tell Brenna about it. She'll appreciate the psychology, if not the killer fish.

I'll tell her, too, about how all the blood-in-the-water parts make me extra paranoid about my period. Or maybe I won't, since that would mean admitting that I'm late. I'm not late enough for it to be an issue, so I probably don't want to make it one. Last thing I want is my doctor checking me out, lecturing me for things I haven't even done. I don't usually skip, and I'm not usually late, but I know that skipping one month doesn't mean anything. Stress can do that, and with everything that's been going on, there's enough stress to count.

On the way home, I realize it's been hours since I thought about work at all.

"Come in for a while?" I ask Andrew when he pulls up in front of my house. He looks at me for a long, searching moment. His hair has dried unevenly and tousled, and the streetlights are picking out the blond and casting shadows, and he looks even more amazing than he always does. Tingle-amazing. I-can't-believe-I'm-with-him amazing. The way he looks at me, it's like he's feeling the same way about me. His gaze makes me feel beautiful.

He shifts into park. "Is everything okay?"

"Yeah… yeah. I'm just not ready to say goodnight yet."

He looks at me a few moments more, as if to make sure I mean it, then leans over and kisses me. "Okay."

We walk hand in hand. Though it's possible to get up the stairs unseen, we detour into the living room to say hi. All three parents are in front of the TV, watching some kind of epic battle with dragons. Andrew raises an eyebrow. His attention is caught. Mine is, too, but it's more fun to tease him than to admit it.

When Dad sees us, he gets up and gives me a tight, wordless hug. Then he claps Andrew on the shoulder with surprising warmth. I don't know what that's about, but it's nice to get affirmation, even the silent kind.

Andrew goes to sit, but I sign "just a minute" and hop upstairs to the linen closet. With folded fresh towels for our butts, I'm willing to sit on the couch in damp swimsuits without fear of parental wrath. We cuddle up, settling in to watch dragons. Andrew's arm tightens around me. I can just barely smell his scent under the strong odor of chlorine.

We all watch together. Dragons breathe fire, they fly effortlessly with their massive, leathery wings, and no man or beast controls them. There's a plot, with kings and queens and politics, but I'm not paying attention to it. Just Andrew's breathing, the comfort of having almost my whole inner circle together in one room being content, and the safety of being surrounded by love. It's the first time I've been able to relax without looking over my shoulder in ages. I want to curl up in this moment and stay here forever.

But all moments end, and so does the dragon movie. Dad gets up, stretching. He comes around behind us and touches Andrew's shoulder again. Then he bends over and kisses the top of my head.

"If it's too late and you're tired, you can crash here," Dad says. "I'd rather that than see anything happen to you on the road, you know?"

Mom and Brenna, who's squinting like she'd fallen asleep, both nod without being prompted.

"Door open," Dad adds. He ruffles my hair and heads upstairs. I want to say something back, but I'm kind of stunned speechless. I'm too stunned to even know if I'm good speechless or bad speechless. I get up to give Mom and Brenna hugs.

"What brought this on?" I murmur in Brenna's ear while our heads are close.

"Accident on the Beltway. A bad one. Two kids, blue Prius, and his heart was in his throat when he drove past. He kept waiting for the call, and you didn't answer when he nudged you."

Our phones were in the locker so they wouldn't get wet or stolen, and I was so distracted I forgot to check mine when I got it back. I try to stammer some of this, but Brenna shakes her head. It's obvious we were swimming just from our current dampness. They've already figured it out.

"Anyway, he's just glad you're safe. Enjoy the permission while you can." She pulls back far enough to wink at me, then follows Mom up the stairs. Now it's just me and Andrew, looking at each other across the dim living room.

"So, um… want to sleep over?" I ask. I try to make it sound like nothing. He holds his hand out. It takes me a moment to realize he wants me to come over to the couch and take it. I do, and he squeezes my fingers, then brings the heel of my palm to his lips.

"Do you want me to?" He doesn't look up at me. Maybe he knows that his gorgeous eyes would bias my answer. "Allie? I'm okay to drive. It's up to you."

I trust myself. I trust him. I'm afraid of the rumor mill. What if someone sees that his car is here all night? But oh my god I miss cuddling with Keisha and falling asleep with her, and if this is a one-time permission thing I'll kick myself forever if I say no to it now.

"I would love for you to stay. But let's agree on how far things can go." I bite my lip. I'm afraid one of us will push things, and not sure which of us it would be. Probably me.

"Okay." Now he looks up, melting me with those eyes. "Listen… I have dry clothes in the car. Why don't I get them, and message my mom, and then we can go upstairs and talk."

I nod, not trusting myself to speak. He stands, kisses me tenderly, and is out the door before I manage to open my eyes from the kiss. It feels like my heart is about to pound its way out of my chest. Part of me is sure this isn't really happening.

When he comes back in, I lock up, then lead the way upstairs. That's easy too, because I already said I was going to. I hear his feet padding up behind me and suddenly there's nothing usual or casual about any of this. It's like I'm climbing toward some big deciding moment. He's been in my room a zillion times, but this time is different.

We stand just inside my door, awkwardly. I clear my throat but I'm not sure what to say.

"So, you take the bathroom and I'll change out here?" he offers.

I nod, relieved to have a sensible plan to follow. The clothes I sleep in are already in there, too. Even better. I start toward the door, stop in my tracks, skip back and kiss him, and then go for real.

I half expect to see the pink sheen of blood when I take off my swimsuit, even despite the moon cup, but it's clean. I pee, then pull out my sanitary device.

Empty. Not a drop. No period.

Considering what's waiting for me on the other side of the door, I don't know whether to be relieved or not. I wash the cup and put it away. Brush teeth. Change into a tank top and sweatpants. Hand on the doorknob, I take a couple of deep breaths.

"Ready or not," I say, opening the door a crack.

"Ready," he answers.

I take a couple steps into the room. Into *my* room. Which has had Andrew in it before. In my bed, kissing me, even. Just not like this.

The door is open Dad's required four inches. Andrew is in a t-shirt and sweats, holding his damp trunks in his hand. I want to run my hands up under his shirt and feel the warmth of his skin.

Not yet.

"There's new toothbrushes in the drawer." I'm stalling. I'm so stalling. But if he sees that, he's kind enough not to let on that he sees it. He squeezes my hand on his way past me.

I turn the overhead light off, pace around awkwardly for a few minutes, then sit on the bed. When Keisha is over, this is "my" side of the bed. Thinking that makes it almost feel wrong to have someone else on "her" side, so I get up and move over. I'm sitting up against the pillows, just finished brushing knots out of my hair when he comes out. He sits beside me, leans in, and kisses me with minty breath.

"We're not going all the way tonight," he says into my hair. "It's not that I don't want to, or that I don't want *you*, but your parents are trusting us with something huge, and I don't want to take advantage of that. I just want you to know that when I do, when I'm ready to, I do want it to be with you."

I swallow hard. My face feels hot. "I want it to be with you, too."

"But not tonight? Is that okay?"

I've never been asked for consent to *not* do something, but I can tell he needs to hear it. He needs to know he's not disappointing me.

He isn't. "That's okay. It's totally okay. I want it to be with you, too, but everything's all upside down right now. For tonight, just having you here to sleep beside is all I want."

He arches an eyebrow. "*All* you want?"

"Shut up," I mutter, pushing at him with the top of my head. He laughs and puts his arms around me. It feels so good to be held. It feels even better to have broken through to the sensitive stuff behind all his innuendo. That's been happening more and more lately, and every time I treasure it as a gift. I know this is an Andrew that most people don't get to see.

We're quiet for a few minutes. I almost start wondering if he's fallen asleep. Then he asks, "So, what happened with Sean?"

I'm tempted to ask him what he's heard, but I don't. There's no answer he could give me that would change how honest I'm going to be with him. "It didn't work out."

"The date, or… ?"

"The date, and."

"Ah," he whispers. "Was it anything in particular?"

I shrug. "I think we're both trying to be close to some part of Keisha, and it's not really about each other."

"That's a mature thing to realize," he says, giving me a squeeze.

"It was an obvious thing. Uncomfortably obvious. Of course, now it means I'm still going to be slut-shamed, it'll just be over multiple boys I'm *not* even dating."

"Oh, you've got company, though. I'm being slut-shamed over him, too." He gives me a rueful grin.

"Ouch. I'm sorry."

"Don't be. It's not your fault. Or your responsibility. You've got it right, you and your family. Nobody can be everything for themselves, much less for anyone else. And look at the world we live in. Anything that brings more love and more stability into this world—how can that be a bad thing?"

I pull back so I can look at him fully. "I love you so much."

His eyes are almost colorless in the dim light from the bathroom. "I love you too, Alicía. Also, I think you're really brave."

"Brave?"

"You're not afraid to be who you are, to be true to yourself. How many of those assholes at the library can say the same? And you inspire me to be true to my feelings, too. This thing that happened with Sean and me? It would be freaking me out if it wasn't for you—for the example you set."

I feel tears threatening, but they're not close. They're like a rumble of thunder in the distance.

"I don't feel brave or strong. I feel like my heart is pulling me apart at the seams. I love you. I love Keisha. I don't get why other people can't understand…" I trail off, sighing. Getting into it is only going to get me worked up and upset, and that's definitely something I don't want to get bogged down in when I have this chance for something special.

"You do, though. You get why, you just don't like that it works that way. Neither do I. But if you change, if you hide, it just makes you miserable and it makes it harder for anyone who comes up that same path after you. 'Cause then the assholes know they can win."

Andrew stretches and looks back at the pillows. I think about what he's just said while I get under the covers and wait for him to join me there. I curl up, safe, with my head on his shoulder and his arm around me. I push his shirt out of the way so that my hand is on his skin.

"What if it threatens my safety to do that? I mean, I'd like to hold the course, but do I have an obligation to sacrifice myself to make a point?"

"No. Of course not. But the other side of that is, you have recourse. You have your parents. They're behind you, and so is the law. If they escalate far enough to threaten your safety. . . harassment is a crime."

"What, you mean tell on Paisley and her assholes? Isn't that a little juvenile?"

"No. It's what adults do when people threaten them. What are you more worried about? That there'll be consequences, or that people won't believe you? Because there's more than enough proof for you to present, and if there's a backlash, it won't be any worse than things are for you right now."

"What about how bad is it upstairs?"

He shrugs. "It's just name calling. It's stupid and harmless, and I'm okay. I promise."

I'm not going to press him on it now. There's a perfect boy in my bed, and even though the door isn't closed and we aren't doing everything, we can still do something. He's never been the one to initiate things, despite talking a big game, but he did ask me what I want, and now I know the answer to that.

"Can I touch you?" I ask, my voice fading to a whisper. "All over?"

He grins, closing his eyes like he's tasting something delicious. "Yes please. Would you like me to touch you all over, too?"

"Please."

"Fingers and hands only?" he asks. I know him. He wants me to say yes so that he can torment me with wanting kisses and other things I've just put out of bounds, but I know he can be maddeningly literal, so I clarify.

"Let the record show that the hands-only restriction is only applicable *below* the waist."

He chuckles. He *was* going to use that to torment me. "Ms. Diaz, I accept your terms."

We do sleep.

Eventually.

I wake up with a body snuggled close to my back, and it takes me a minute to convince myself that last night wasn't just a dream. That I'm not still dreaming now.

In a way, it all makes sense. If my parents know what I get up to with Keisha, and they *must* know, a sleepover with a boy isn't any more scandalous. If anything, *less* happened with Andrew. Go figure.

I stretch as best I can without disturbing Andrew. He shifts when I do, draping his arm over my waist. I take his hand and hug it to my body. I know he's awake when he draws it up that small remaining distance and cups my breast. It's a lazy gesture, twice as hot because it's so casual and natural. The curve of me fits just right in the curve of his palm.

It's tempting to rock my hips back against him, but in the light of morning I'm much more conscious of the open door than I was in the dark. Reluctantly, I pull his hand from its cozy spot and bring it up to my lips. I nibble on the soft pad of a fingertip. He murmurs something unintelligible, so I keep nibbling.

If this was anyone else's house, I'd expect a surprise inspection to make sure we're clothed and on good behavior, but my parents either trust people or they don't. They don't lay traps to test them.

Andrew feels around my face until he finds my nose, taps it while whispering "boop," and retrieves his hand. His fingers ease through my hair. I roll over, toward him. His eyes are warm, and as gentle as his smile.

"Hi," I whisper.

"Mmm. Hi."

"Sleep okay?"

"You know..." He shrugs one shoulder. "First night in a new bed. Good dreams, though."

"Me, too." I can feel myself grinning. I feel like a dork.

He props up on his elbow. "Do you mind if I shower? I feel like pool crud."

Imagining him naked in my shower, soaping himself in places that I know the feel of now, is a little more than my willpower can handle, but I try to rein it in. "Sure. I'll go on downstairs, so they don't think we're showering together."

It feels weird leaving him alone in my room. Also, I'm not ready to stop touching him. Once he's closed the bathroom door, it's easier to leave.

Downstairs, muffins are baking. Coffee is ready. Ozone is begging at Brenna's feet, rearing up on his hind legs to sniff at the empty hand she offers him. "Nothing. See?"

He spots me and makes a beeline for me, twining around my ankles and rubbing his face—and wet nose—all over my legs. "I don't have any food either. Sorry!"

I pour milk, add coffee, and cradle the mug in my palms. It's blue-glazed pottery, probably older than me, and I know it's handmade but I've never been able to decipher the artist's marks in the bottom.

"Where's the boy?" she asks.

"In the shower. By himself." Why did I add that? Now my cheeks are burning.

"Glad to be your alibi," she says with a grin.

"No, your honor, I was with Brenna the whole time!" I look to her for approval and get a thumbs up. "It's not like we *need* to get our story straight. Apparently you all trust me more with a penis than you trust me with a car."

She smirks, considering this. "Well, to be fair, you haven't crashed any penises."

CHAPTER 14

It turns out, getting coffee out of your sinuses is a lot harder than getting coffee into them. Brenna and I mostly get everything back in order before anyone else comes downstairs. That's because the thing that summons them all, apparently, is the scent of muffins. "I'll get them," I tell Brenna when the timer goes off. "Don't worry, I've never crashed an oven."

She laughs, holds her sides, and flops into a chair. I'm glad she can joke around with me like this, without watching her words or holding them back.

The pan is cooling on the counter when everybody else arrives, led by their noses. Dad pulls me into a hug on his way to coffee. No one asks why the floor is a little damp in spots, and Brenna and I don't volunteer.

I'm not sure what it is about morning that draws people out of themselves. Maybe we're less inhibited because we're less awake. Maybe we're willing to admit we're tumbled-up on the inside because everyone else is tumbled-up on the outside.

Breakfast isn't a formal thing at our house. It sprawls from the kitchen to the living room, more of a slow waking-up over coffee than anything else. Even now, though we're all in the same room, it's a help-yourself, socialization-optional kind of thing.

"Have you guys ever gotten push-back over your relationship?" Andrew asks my parents. "Or have people not really cared, on the whole?"

I haven't talked with any of them about our recent difficulties at the library. I can't tell if he's leading up to mentioning that or not.

"We didn't all live together until we moved here—so, not until Alicía started high school," Mom says. "We don't try to hide it, but we've never been affectionate in public, so it's never really been an issue. What brings this on? Anything specific?"

"Not specific. I just don't really have any other people with experience to talk to about it. Is this okay?" Andrew asks. "I mean… I mean, personal questions first thing in the morning?"

Dad sets his tablet aside, to show he's paying attention. "Sure. Of course."

"So… the books talk a lot about equal partners versus primaries and secondaries. I can get that, at our age, being all on the same level, but how do you decide who to live with, or who to marry? What does that do to things like legal rights, or visiting in the hospital—like when it's family only? And there are all sorts of bedroom things that are still illegal in this state." He turns to Brenna. "Do you ever say you're Allie's stepmom, just to make things easier?"

I'm still stuck way back at the beginning of all that, at the "books" part. I'm touched and flattered that he's gone out of his way to research our relationship. Though I suppose I'm not actually all that surprised.

"I'm Allie's godmother," Brenna says, "so if we need to play gymnastics then I can say I'm a legal guardian. Technically, godparents are considered to be the next caretakers in line if anything happens to the parents, so especially now that we have the same address, that usually works fine. I'm listed that way at school, for instance, so I can sign Allie out or call her in absent just like her birth parents can."

I knew all this, but I never really thought about it. Andrew nods, his expression distant with that look that means he's processing everything he's just heard.

"As for the bedroom…" Dad says, and I don't know how he says it so matter-of-factly, "we all have separate rooms here, so anyone who wanted to point fingers at what we were or weren't doing in private in our own home, would have a hard time of it. And as for marriage, we always insisted it was something we'd never do. But then, long story short, it came down to an issue of needing health insurance. Maria and I were living together, and our other partners—though just as important—are both women, so I was the groom elect. Everyone agreed they'd rather see Maria healthy than unmarried and sick, or in debt for life, so they insisted."

"And when I got better, we celebrated and I got pregnant," Mom concludes. "But it wasn't like it was a planned thing, where I got the pedestal because I had the baby. It just sort of worked out to look that way."

"There was no strategic 'mothering initiative committee,' no," Dad says with a faint smirk. We've stumbled on an inside joke that I don't want to understand.

"And marrying the Latina girlfriend instead of the white girl went a long way toward mending things with your parents," Brenna reminds Dad.

Dad shrugs. "Well, true, but that didn't factor big in my decision. I decided when I was eighteen that whether they accepted me or not was something I couldn't try to control. I'd never live my life if I spent it worrying what other people thought, Abi and Belo included."

I don't know if Andrew knows about Dad's name change or Mom's surgery. It's nothing scandalous or anything: she ignored the pain in her appendix until it got really bad, because she was a grad student and her insurance would have made her pay more than she could afford. She's more annoyed at the state of health care in this country than ashamed or embarrassed, these days.

"Here's the thing about books," Brenna says. She lists off a few titles and Andrew nods to a couple of them. They must be the ones he's read. "Most of them should be in the philosophy section, not in psychology or self-help."

So, 150.1, I think: that's where Dewey Decimals puts psychological philosophy and theory. I keep my mouth shut.

"If you approach them as theory," Brenna continues, "they're fine. Theory is interesting and good to learn. Just keep in mind, none of these books are the practical instruction guides people want them to be. At best, they're pure thought-experiment, and they own up to it. At worst, they're wish-fulfillment—they're written about what people wish their relationships were like, not what they're actually like. All the problem solving they demonstrate? That's what they wish they could have done, in hindsight. It's often not a road-map for what actually worked."

"So when people treat this stuff as instructions…"

"Right. It doesn't always work like painting by numbers. Then you feel like you must be the one getting it wrong, and you start questioning your partners—maybe *they're* the ones doing it wrong—and it's a hard climb back up to communicating and trusting your instincts."

"Brenna knows of what she speaks," Mom says, then looks at her expectantly.

Brenna rolls her eyes and sighs, universal language for *fine, I'll tell the story.*

"Before they moved out here," Brenna tells Andrew, "I was involved briefly with an author of one of those books. We met at a conference and I admired all the positivity in his book and his interviews. He seemed to have it all figured out. Well, we kept in touch, things progressed in hopeful ways, but after about ten minutes of watching him navigate his relationships at home, I could see that he didn't live as he preached. At all. The conflicts he described in his books were real, but the way they were resolved was all idealized. You know how sometimes you ask a question online and half the people who answer don't actually know, they just tell you what their assumption is, as if it's fact?"

"Like when you ask how often the trains run on Sunday nights," Andrew says. "Oh, they *should* run every fifteen minutes." It sounds like he's quoting from wry experience.

"Exactly. It *should*, not *it does*. Not even 'I think it does, but can someone else check, because the schedule might be different on Sundays.'"

"The difference between theory and practice…" Dad adds, "is that in theory, there's no difference."

"No plan survives contact with the enemy," Mom agrees. "People are totally predictable, except when they're not."

"Hearts are jerks," Brenna and I say at the same time. She offers me a fist bump across the table.

"Anyway," Brenna says. "The point is not 'this one guy wrote a book of lies, so all authors are lying liars.' The point is, I got to see inside this guy's life and it put a completely different context to his advice. Now I'm always aware, when I read advice, that I don't know the context behind it. I don't know if it's true experience or hindsight or pure theory. Whatever they're suggesting you do, it's an option to consider, but it's not something that necessarily even worked for the person suggesting it, and I've got a different family of people who bring different history and circumstances, and different personalities to the mix, and have different needs."

Andrew absorbs this. "Like whether there are children involved, or whether one partner is long distance," he says, and Brenna nods. "So, good exposure to theory and hypothetical situations, but in the end it all still comes down to…"

"Remember that what a person tells you they need is always more important than what a book or website tells you they're supposed to need."

"And listen, and have empathy."

"And be kind," Dad says. His phone buzzes and he sneaks a look at it. "Carry on," he says, getting up. "Good stuff going on here, but I need to take this."

"Totally having an affair," Mom deadpans when Dad leaves the room. Brenna and I laugh. Andrew looks at us like he's amazed we can joke about such things. I reach out and squeeze his hand.

"So, does cheating just not exist, when… ?"

"Oh, cheating totally exists," Brenna says. "You have rules and expectations in any relationship. There are still rules that can be broken, they're just not always the same as other people's rules. It's not funny because it's impossible, it's funny because it's unnecessary. Jeff wouldn't have to cheat. If he was interested in someone, we'd probably both cheer him on."

Did I cheat on Keisha? We didn't have a rule that I wouldn't mess around with other people, whether they were her boyfriend or anyone else. But all the same, by this point I can't tell myself I just haven't had a chance to bring it up. It's gone beyond that. I know I'm actively hiding it. I really need to ask Sean what he's said to her about it, but that means talking to Sean. I'm not ready for that yet.

Andrew has to go home eventually. I walk him to his car. "This was the best date ever," I murmur into his shoulder. He hugs me tight.

"Let's do it again soon," he agrees. "See you tomorrow?"

Tomorrow is work. Prep class. Stress. "Yup. I've been warned about being huggy at work, so I probably shouldn't… you know."

"I know. It's okay." He makes a sign with his fingers. "Here. The letter k, for kissing you from across the room."

"Mmm. You think of everything."

He gets in and starts the car. Across the street, the curtains twitch. That's Loudon Quinn's room. We're not exactly friends, but it's not like we're enemies. It shouldn't affect me, then, if she's watching me and Andrew say goodbye. I mean, what's it to her? But it's a sign of how paranoid I am that it gets to me anyway. What, like she's going to go post about how he spent the night?

That's exactly what she does. My inner paranoid voice was right. Not only is it validated, but I think it's actually gloating at me. I hate when I've finally gotten my self-doubt to settle down and I've got a more reasonable story to tell myself about what's going on, and then it turns out my worst fear was right anyway. Yeah, yeah, maybe instinct and intuition are there for a reason. They can still shut up.

And so can Loudon Quinn.

When you post a video blog, you can just film yourself talking about anything. Any opinion you have, any rant you want to go off on. People can leave comments, but it's not like posting text and having a conversation in the comments. It's more encapsulated, less open to editing or interpretation, and if you already have your own echo chamber, it can go viral really quickly.

"Oh my god, you guys. Check out the house of debauchery across the street. That's Andrew Novak's car, and it's been outside Allie Diaz's house all night. So not only are her parents having weird perverted threesomes, and possibly running a sex ring out of their basement—I see a *lot* of different cars come and go from that house all day long—but they're encouraging their daughter now, too. Look!" The camera pans to the window, to me and Andrew saying goodbye. "He *has* been in there all night. Oh my god, they're all gross. I hear she's been cozying up with two guys and they both know about each other. So be careful, boys. She might seem like a sure thing, but there's a few too many horses at that watering hole, if you know what I mean. Like, starting with fluid-borne disease, right? And look at her. She can't possibly be worth the risk. Ugh." The curtains close in disgust and the screen goes blank.

My face feels cold and my hands are burning. Or maybe it's the other way around. The video already has almost two hundred views. I close it out. It feels like I'm trying to think through bubble wrap: it's disorienting and obscuring, but I'm really glad it's there.

There was something I was going to... oh, email. There's nothing in my inbox except some kind of stupid dating site spam. I'm getting more of it than usual. I never pay much attention to it, but there's enough to be noticeable. I'll update my filters soon. For now, I just delete it all unread. I've missed a phone call from my dad—that one, I know about—but also four from a number that isn't in my contacts. Keisha's probably not even awake yet, but I message her a photo of me in my pajamas. Today doesn't feel like it's worth getting dressed for.

As the video spreads through my peer group, I get a few messages of support. Andrew sends me love and hugs, and reminds me not to give in to the temptation to engage. Of course it's bullshit; of course there are a lot of people who come and go at the house. Brenna's a counselor, seeing her clients. And Loudon knows that, because her brother went to Brenna for a while when he came back from deployment. There was an article in the local paper where he talked about it, and everything.

The whispering and giggling were one thing. This is on a completely different level. I'm not a violent person, but I really want to march across the street and punch Loudon in the face. With my luck, she'd be recording that, too.

My phone rings, startling me. It's Keisha.

"Hey. Good morning," I say.

"Hey. What the hell crawled up Loudon's butt?"

"I don't know. I mean, kids being assholes is one thing, but..."

"But what did your parents ever do to her?"

I sigh, I don't want to get into the whole library morality police thing, but it's part of the same harassment picture, so I do.

"Wow. Who dumped hate in the water out there?" she asks when I finish. "Shit. Has anyone threatened your safety?"

I think about that guy grabbing my pool float, but that's not what she means. She means have any guys tried to take a turn. "No. Nothing like that."

"Yet. Be careful, okay? Don't let anyone corner you alone."

"I'll be careful. How about you? How's *your* drama?"

She snerks. "Right? At least my drama is stuff I signed up for. It's good. Hard but good. Everyone here is way serious about all this."

"Well, so are you, right?"

"Yeah. I guess I just never realized how far from big league I am. I mean, it's good to know now, while I have time to skill up. It's just, I'm trying to learn things that can't be taught, so…"

"Yeah."

A knock distracts me. Dad's at my door, looking expectant. "I gotta go. I love you. Call me back later if you want. I'll be here."

When she hangs up, I feel twice as lonely as I did when I could hear her voice. I wish we'd had time to video-chat. I wish she could be here to hug all this stupidity away. But wishing doesn't make anything happen.

"What's up, Dad?"

"I need to borrow your phone for a minute. Time to update a firmware setting."

I hand it over. "I'm capable of hitting the 'okay' button too, you know," I tease him. I know that when he has phone updates, they're security measures he has to install because of his government job. I don't know details, just that our home wifi and everything that attaches to it has to be extra secure.

He disappears with the phone. I poke around my room for a while, then make my bed. It's an excuse to hug the pillow that still smells like Andrew.

I check my laptop. The video is up to 500 views.

When Dad returns with my phone, he's wearing his concerned face. I panic for a moment, but there's literally nothing bad in there that he could have found. No sexts or secrets or compromising photos. The most out-there pics I have are some empty jeans and blurry elbows.

"What's wrong?" I ask as I take it back.

"Are other kids giving you grief, Allie?"

I hesitate, swaying on my feet a little, like a character in a video game waiting idly while you figure out what to have them do next. "A little," I say finally, and try to shrug it off. "I hugged two boys, so now I'm a slut. And Loudon, across the street, posted something mean this morning when she saw that Andrew's car was still here. It'll pass, though. It's summer and they're bored."

He frowns; he doesn't seem reassured at all. I don't want to tell him that it's all part of Paisley's hate campaign because I hit her dead grandparents with the car and then had coffee with her brother. Having Dad step into the middle of that will just make it more complicated—she's not *personally* doing anything to me, not in any tangible, punishable way… and if she knows how much she's getting to me, she'll just ramp things up.

I don't know what to say that might make things better, so I change gears. "Thanks for letting Andrew stay over. It was nice to—I mean, I really appreciate your trust."

"He's a good kid, and so are you." He pats me on the shoulder and turns to go.

"Wait. Dad, what's this about?"

He turns back, measuring me for a second. "I trust you. Will you trust me?"

Mutely, I nod.

"Good," he says. "I'll explain when I can, but for now, the less you know. Okay?"

"Okay," I say, because it has to be. "Three questions? Yes/no?"

He considers it. "Two."

"One: Is this about the car?"

"No."

"Is it about catching someone who broke the law?"

He has to think for a second, so maybe that means I've picked a good question. "Yes. Don't open anything from anyone you don't know or trust."

I've been hearing—and following—that advice for as long as I've been allowed on the internet, so I agree like I always do. Meanwhile, I'm imagining spy stuff from the movies. Maybe my phone is set to ping Dad's office when I'm next to a bank robber on the subway, so the police can be waiting for him when the doors open. That could be kind of exciting. More likely, it's something boring. Probably, someone's tried to crack our home firewall, so he wants me extra shielded against hacker code that someone might try to slip into my phone through a spam mail.

For the next week, I keep my head down at work. I don't talk to Andrew at the library, and I don't rise to it when boys ask me which aisle they can find a blowjob in, or girls talk about me right in front of me. I don't rise to it when Paisley goes to hand me a book and then drops it with a smirk before I can take it from her. I delete all my spam mail without looking at it. I don't read the comments on Loudon's video blog, or look at the new videos on her stream.

Cecil comes by the library again, picking up Paisley, and makes her wait while he says hi to me and tries to make oblivious small talk. She stands impatiently behind him, and the look on her face could melt flesh. It's confirmation, for me. This isn't just about the gravestone, but it's about her brother liking me, too. That's why she and her friends are all making so much of the slut angle. It's not only because they think it's the easiest way to get me fired, it's more personal than that. I gently tell Cecil that his sister is waiting on him and I have to get back to work, but somehow I'm still the villain for having distracted him in the first place—Paisley sneers at me before they turn to go.

A week turns into two. Independence Day comes and goes. I could go downtown to watch the D.C. fireworks live with Andrew and his mom and Sean, but I still don't think I have anything to say to Sean. I choose to watch the pyrotechnics on television with my parents. I send Keisha a selfie and tell her I miss her. She sends a photo back: she's on a beach with fireworks and a huge crowd, because of course she is. I wish I was with her.

A whole month of work probation and juvenile prodding goes by. And for whatever it's worth, I still haven't gotten my period.

CHAPTER 15

A the end of July, on pay day, my probation is lifted. No one actually tells me, but there's a letter tucked in the envelope beside my check. When I open it, finding printed type on county letterhead, I fear the worst. I read through it again, making sure the news is still good.

It's snatched out of my hands. Paisley twirls away from me, reading while she spins. It's hard to grab the page back from a moving target; this is something she's learned from having a sibling, no doubt, whereas I've never had to learn how to outsmart one. I have to wait for her to stop and return the letter. My hands are shaking and I'm not sure I'll be able to get the page back in the envelope as gracefully as I'd like to, so I shove both in my bag separately. Whatever.

"Not that it's any of your business," I say.

She flips her hair. "It is now. Someone's got to protect the children." Her voice is sharp and malicious. This isn't just something she's heard an adult say.

I turn away before I can say anything I can regret. I'm supposed to get a moment of relief now that one stress—the fear of losing my job—has been eased, but she's stolen that moment from me. Or at least, that's how it feels. Really, she hasn't stolen anything. That moment is mine to take. I'll just postpone it a little.

I feel even sicker when I see Paisley in the back talking to Faith, who's one of Loudon's friends, and showing her something on her phone.

They might be discussing Loudon's stupid video blogs, the ones that call my whole family sluts. Andrew looked up the case law and said it's not actionable, legally, unless Brenna can prove she's losing clients over it, and so far she isn't. I think about all the times I've talked myself out of the worst possible explanations for things, only to find out that my instinct had been right after all. I'm not doing that today.

Not even for my period.

Show's over, body. Back to work! I think. I know stress can delay it, but for it to be delayed by stress over it being delayed, that would just be cruel and unusual. If it takes much longer, I'm going to have to get checked out.

I'm terrified of having to explain to a doctor that yes, I'm still a virgin with guys, and also at the same time, no, I don't know whose it might be. Having to defend myself about that is even more terrifying than pregnancy. I need to suck it up. Denial is much more comfortable, but I don't want to hit some kind of point of no return where it's too late to have options.

I open a search window on my phone, and type *can you get pregnant from*. The autocomplete suggestions are "precum," "oral," "grinding"—I pick that one and long-press to hover over the link and see the preview text. *Can you get pregnant from grinding?*

No, the internet says, the chance of it is extremely low, especially with clothes in the way, because there's almost no way for a sperm to find its way into the vaginal canal from outside and through two layers of underwear.

"Almost no way" isn't as comforting as it's probably meant to be.

I need to be able to make my own decision. You know, if.

I wish I didn't have to face this by myself. Who can I tell, though?

Not Andrew. He'd have too much invested in the outcome. Not my parents. They've trusted me with Andrew and Keisha, and I've worked hard to keep earning and justifying that trust. That leaves Keisha, who I didn't even tell about that whole grinding incident in the first place. I can't lead into it with this.

I don't think there's an age restriction on buying a pregnancy test. The longer it's in the house the more chance someone's going to find it, so that would make me use it right away. I could ask Keisha to hold my virtual hand while I take it. She's good at keeping me calm, and maybe she'd know what to do. I could do that detail-omission thing again, and she'd assume I was worried about just Andrew. I feel a flush of relief and guilt in equal measure. It's a plan, at least. She'd probably be more pissed if I didn't include her. We have to work at not making the other feel left out, that's something Mom said, and Keisha is still my girlfriend, isn't she? But she'd feel left out because we messed around without her. Either way, there's leaving out, but I think continuing to dodge would be worse. I'll own up.

Now there's just the matter of where to buy it. Nowhere I'm a regular, obviously. Nowhere that I'd need someone to drive me. Not online. That doesn't leave me many options, but some extra leg work is worth it if it means keeping my shopping trip from showing up in one of Loudon's videos.

For the last month, Andrew's known we can't talk while I'm at work. I probably forgot, with everything else going on, to tell him that my probation was lifted, so he leaves without stopping by the desk, only making the little sign at me that we agreed was kissing from afar. By the time I remember how to sign "wait," he's already gone.

It's raining in the morning, so I ask Brenna for a ride to work. Then I ask if she minds waiting while I duck into the drugstore for a new phone case. She hangs out in the car while I run in. I pick up a cheap case, a pregnancy test, and also nail polish and nail polish remover, tights, and a school year planner. Basically, all things I can hide the test between when I come out.

I'm positive the bored clerk guy is giving me side-eye. Maybe I should have picked weirder stuff to go with the pregnancy test, like tweezers and a metal detector and a bunch of tabloids with cover stories about alien abduction, like Keisha used to do with the library books. I'm not feeling that clever right now, though. I'm feeling a lot of things, but clever isn't one of them.

I get back into the car with the ten-cent plastic bag on my lap. I'm pretty sure the test is burning a hole in it.

"Success?" Brenna asks me.

"Yup. I went a little binge-crazy."

"You deserve it. Anything good?"

"Glitter for my nails. Nothing too interesting."

She glances toward the bag, so I feel around in it and pull out the polish. The bottle is full of floating pieces of holographic glitter in a base that's the same pale blue as Andrew's eyes.

"Oh, nice. I might ask to borrow that. Manicure party after work? I can pick you up tonight, and we can stop off and get donut holes."

We haven't done that since I was a little kid, but right now it sounds comforting and awesome. "It's a date."

All day, I can't quite forget that a pregnancy test is waiting for me, silently judging me for being too chicken to use it.

I want to tell it to go to hell, but I don't want to make it angry, as if it's a sentient thing that understands English and intentions. As if my disdain has anything in the world to do with the outcome. "Not today," I tell it instead. "You should be happy. You've evaded urine for another day."

I hang out downstairs with the family all evening, but I can feel its presence weighing on me. The Tell-Tale Pee Stick. Wouldn't it be better just to know? To have options?

I keep glancing at the time. We watch cheesy movies until we're all falling asleep, and then trundle off to bed. I can't keep my eyes open downstairs, but once I'm snug between my sheets, everything that's been lulled in my head comes back at full volume. I shut my eyes resolutely and refuse to acknowledge the test in the drawer, or anything but the safety of my room and the feel of the pillow against my cheek.

It doesn't help.

I drag myself out of bed to take an anxiety pill. On my way back from the bathroom, I stop at my desk, where I stashed the test when I got home.

Better just to know. Better to have options.

I take my phone and the cardboard box into the bathroom and set them both on the counter. I read the instructions on the box, then open it. That's a task in itself. Then, inside, the test itself is in a sealed foil wrapper, and inside that there's a tape seal around the edge of the cover that protects the pee stick. I've seen bank heist movies where the vault was less protected than this. I feel absolutely safe that no one has ever peed on this stick before.

I'm supposed to hold the end of it in urine for five seconds. I don't know if I have five seconds worth of pee in me, so I grab a paper cup. I'll pee in that instead, and dip the stick into it for a count of five.

I position the cup, wait… and wait some more. Am I actually too nervous to go?

I turn the faucet on and concentrate on the sound of water running and dripping. That helps, and soon my bladder releases. I go a little, then bring the cup in the way. That's how they tell you to do it at the doctor's office. "Mid-stream" pee, not like it's going to make a difference in this case.

After the cup is safely on the counter, I start unwrapping the cover from the stick.

The entire counter vibrates. For a second, I wonder if I've triggered some sort of anti-theft something. Then I realize it's my phone, with Keisha's photo on the screen. It takes a couple more buzzes for me to catch my breath and answer.

"Hi?"

"Hi, Allie." I hear her inhale, then sigh. "Shit. It's probably really late there, isn't it? I just needed to hear your voice. The shit-stirrers are stirring shit, and I feel so isolated out here, it's hard to know what's real and what's just stirred up."

"Ugh. What's the latest?"

"They made it sound like you were bragging about screwing Sean and then ghosting him, like someone dared you to. It made me think about how you haven't mentioned him at all, and all I've heard from him was that you cut things off abruptly. I know the pieces don't all fit, but I don't have enough of them to make another picture instead, you know?"

I'm wincing the whole time she's talking, and it's all I can do to keep myself from interrupting her, but I hold my tongue and let her finish.

"I haven't had sex with him. Not with either of them. We all messed around one time, the three of us," I tell her. "Like you and me and Andrew did once or twice. Had he told you that?"

"Yeah. Video games and consoling each other. He told me that. I kept waiting for *you* to tell me."

"I'm sorry I kept you waiting. Now I know how you felt, not telling me about the move right away. There was never a good moment."

"I think I picked up on your guilt, or discomfort or whatever, though," she says. "Maybe that primed me to believe shit?"

"Maybe," I agree limply. I have no defense for this, and I'm not going to make excuses for myself. "There's been a lot of shit, and I miss you like crazy, and it's all been upside down, all summer. I'm so sorry you had to see those stupid video blogs, and that people dragged you into it. You have enough to deal with." I laugh, weakly. "I don't even know what you've had to deal with, because we haven't had any time for you to tell me."

"Yeah. Stupid time zones. By the time I'm out of rehearsal, you're in bed. Speaking of bed, where are you? You've got a weird echo."

I glance around. In the rush to take her call, I haven't finished the things I came into the bathroom to do. I'm still on the toilet, staring at the purple towel on the rack attached to the opposite wall. I tell her so.

"Okay. Whyyyyy?" She drags out the question word, as if it's strange to be on the phone from the toilet in the middle of the night.

Sometimes the only way to say something is to take a deep breath and blurt. "I'm two months late so I'm peeing on a stick."

There's a moment's silence while she processes that. "Oh, honey. Have you gone yet?"

I look over at the counter. "I'm a dork. It's sitting here in a cup. I was just about to do the stick part when you called."

"We'll do it together, okay?" she says.

She's just offered me exactly what I was afraid to ask for, and without any prompting or fishing from me. Because she wants to; because she cares.

"Okay." I set the phone down, put it on speaker, and turn the volume down so that her amplified voice doesn't travel through the house. Then I uncap the test stick. I'm supposed to put it in for five seconds, and then wait up to five minutes for results.

I submerge it, and we count together. The wick-like part absorbs the pee and turns orange-pink with it, which is disconcerting even though I know that pinkness there doesn't mean positive. I close it up, set it down, and peer at its screen.

"Well?" Keisha asks.

"There's a minus already. Does the whole thing go at the same time, or does the other line develop at a different speed?"

"How do I know?" she counters. "But I think it's all at once."

"Tell me about your week, while I keep an eye on it?"

She chuckles softly, and even though it isn't meant to be sultry, it's a sound I remember feeling like a purr when she'd do it close to my ear. "Thought you'd never ask."

A late night on the phone is followed by an early morning. There's a knock on my door, and Mom peeks in. "Can I use your bathroom? It's kind of urgent."

"I… No! I mean—" I'm on my feet before I realize I'm getting up. "I mean, let me pick it up first. It's a mess. There's… jungle beasts. Chemical spill. Toxic. And… spiders. Really big spiders. Chemical spill *and* spiders. They might have powers!" But at this point I'm just trailing behind her and I know there's nothing I can do to stop her.

She shuts the door. I wring my hands and wait. A flush, a rush of water in the sink, and she comes out, still wiping her hands on a purple towel.

"I think a spider bit me. I'm overcome with a sudden need to hear truth," she says gently. "Can you help me?"

We sit on the foot of my bed. After all that work to keep the test hidden, I left it on the counter in plain sight, figuring I'd clean it up in the morning.

I tell her about being two months late, and about video game night. Not all the details, but enough. She believes me, that things didn't go all the way. That's a blessing and a curse. Being believed, that is. It's awesome that my parents trust me, but it also makes me feel stupid, like I've been suffering over here for the hell of it when I could have gone to them at any time.

She doesn't ask the question I'm dreading. Maybe it'll be easier if I don't wait for it, so I do that deep-breath-and-blurt thing that worked so well last night. "You make it look so easy, all of you. Like you've got it all solved. Whenever I have trouble and I come to you, you have answers for me. Which, I mean, it's great that you can help me, but it makes me feel like these things have already been figured out and I'm some kind of impossibly slow screw-up. So I can't come to you.

I have to figure it out on my own, because clearly there *are* answers if you all know them already."

We've had this conversation before, more than once. We started to have it on the stairs, that day I sent Sean home. But I don't think I've ever told her how it makes me feel.

Mom pulls me close. "You are absolutely justified if you want to forge your own path. I support you. We all do. We've earned our answers through our own blood and tears, and our answers might not even be yours. You might find better ones. You've already encountered things that we never have, just like we've lived through persecution for things that are taken for granted now. All the advice I've ever given you has been from a place of my own experience; your mileage may vary. I've always thought that was understood. I apologize for not realizing that it wasn't. We definitely don't have the answers, but our insight is all yours, anytime you want it." She laughs faintly; I feel it through her chest. "We're your library, and our doors will never be closed to you."

"Do I have to stamp you with Dewey numbers? Because that could get awkward."

She squeezes me. "*Mija*, if it made you feel better, I'd let you. Just don't put me on the same shelf as your dad."

I pull back and we look at each other. And we both add, "He snores."

Mom brushes a stray curl away from my face—curls I got from her. "Listen. You love who you love. Don't let anyone shame you for that. Don't ever wish it was different, or that you could turn off those feelings just to fit in better. But don't scorn people who aren't brave enough yet to do what you do. If you push them, they'll just run away."

"To Chicago?" It's just a guess, but the way she sighs tells me it's a good guess.

"Here, I have experience, but not answers. My heart loves someone who wishes she didn't love women. It tears her up. Keisha, at least, accepts it in her heart. It might take her until she's living on her own to show it to the world, but the reality we live in is that some parents *do* still withdraw support from their children based on who they love or who they are. Don't make my mistake and fault her for protecting herself."

I nod. Words don't come, because I've never seen this side of her before. They really don't have all the answers. They really do still go through the weaknesses and the pains. It says a lot that after all these years, she's still trying to make it work with Tina, still loving her on Tina's terms.

"Your heart's a jerk, too?" I ask her, finally.

"Big, big jerk. So if you find any answers…"

"I'll be an open library, too." And, because I don't remember the last time I said it: "I love you. And your jerk heart."

She touches her forehead to my forehead, then her nose to my nose. "I love you and your jerk heart, too. Even when you don't clean your bathroom."

This close, I can't stop her from seeing me blush. My embarrassment makes her grin. "If that's what it takes to make this happen," I counter, "maybe I should leave it messy more often."

She pulls back, ruffling my hair like Dad does. "I'm going to pretend your brain didn't mean that. Clean it up now, or I'll make sure you get two more of these talks."

Mom has a big heart, but she's still a mom.

The next day at work, I'm feeling better about things. I'm definitely not pregnant, my mom's pep talk has given me a lot of hope about relationships, and it's given me a new look into my parents' humanity. Whatever resentment I've been carrying around feels gone, or at least lighter.

It doesn't even particularly bother me to see Paisley and Faith in the stacks, making those giggle-snort noises you make when you're trying really hard to stop laughing. Their heads are bowed over a phone so close that their hairspray might stick them together, and they're whispering. I'm so intently focused on trying to read their lips that I don't notice the man until he's almost standing on me.

"Allie?" he asks.

I squint up at him. He looks like he's my parents' age, dressed in khakis and a polo shirt. It's the sort of outfit a teacher might wear.

"I'm sorry?" I try not to stammer, in case he's someone important.

"Hi. I'm Vince. KindEyes38? You look just like your profile. Wow." He smiles, then looks around. "So, where did you want to do it?"

I blink. Um… "I'm sorry, but… what?" There's no context to even try to fit this into. If he's a college recruiter here for an interview, it's weird to introduce himself with an online handle. I glance at his eyes and they are pretty kind. Not beady or bloodshot or anything. Maybe he's from the cemetery, or from the library board or something. But even if he is, why a screen name? And what would he be here to "do," right now while I'm working? Interviewing me? I don't have all the money yet, and anyway why would he come to me and not to Dad?

"Cold feet? I thought you said it was your fantasy to —" he cuts short, glances around, and drags me by the upper arm into the aisle between the newspapers and the books on tape. His voice drops to a whisper. "You said you wanted to suck a stranger's dick in the stacks. I snuck away from work for this. So what's wrong? You were lively enough on chat last night."

It's starting to… not to make *sense*, exactly, but to at least form a coherent picture.

"I'm sorry. I don't know what you're talking about." I try to pull my arm away. He lets go once he realizes I mean it and I'm likely to scream. "I—maybe someone used my picture for something? It's shitty that someone got your hopes up, but I'm sorry. I swear it wasn't me."

"Come on, Alison, don't be that way." He plucks at my arm again. "You know it's what you want."

My mind's racing. "Show me. Show me where I said that."

He sighs, fishes his phone out of his pocket, and pulls up an image to show me.

It's a chat screen, inside some kind of dating app. Whoever Alliecat is, she's got my face appending each message.

If I play dumb and resist, you'll just have to drag me into the men's room and fuck me there. My safeword is paleoanthropology. As long as I don't say that word, you can take me however you want as long as we don't get caught.

My eyes fill with angry tears. Pretending to set me up for a date: ha ha. Arranging to get me raped? At work? What kind of shit is that?

I glance around, but I don't see anyone. They've got to be watching. Filming. They're not going to help me. There's no Keisha, no Andrew. It's just me. If someone's going to save me, it's going to have to be me.

Think fast. Think fast.

If I use that safeword now, he'll leave. I want him to leave, more than anything, but I also want consequences for whoever thought this would be funny.

"So... I have this friend who works here. She'll stand watch for us, but you have to show her that message so she knows you're the right guy. Okay?"

I'm ready to point out that someone might call the cops if we don't have an ally, but there's no need. His eyes aren't kind anymore. They're hard and full of purpose. He nods and turns to follow me, his hand a lead weight on my shoulder. Now I just have to hope this works.

I take him into the back. Dee's not here today, and why would she be? She's the supervisor of all the libraries in the county so she travels around a lot, but I know she's in my corner, as much as anyone is. Without her, that leaves me only one option and it's a long shot that she'll even believe me.

"Hey, Janice?" I cringe at how nervous I sound. She looks up from her desk.

"Show her your phone," I tell Vince, trying to smile. "She's on that site too. Her screen name is CodePurple."

That's the code for "I am under duress" or "violent person in the building." I've never been so grateful for those boring monthly drills.

"Purple's my favorite color. It's all I write in," Janice says, and I know that when she pulls her purple felt tip pen out of her desk drawer to show him, she's also hitting the panic button. The outer door is now locked and won't open till the police get here. Five minutes, tops. The station is only a few blocks away, so maybe three minutes. That's 180 seconds. That's nothing. I could count that.

"So, let's see this," she says, and the Vince guy lets go of me and hands the phone over. I can see her eyes go hard as she reads. She's careful not to look at me, because he might catch whatever passes between us and know we're stalling him while help arrives. If we make a fuss and call him a freak, he'll try to run. If he can't run, there's a chance he could get dangerous instead. Or try to erase it from his phone, leaving me without proof.

"Shame on you, missy," Janice says. "There's a typo in here. That's not like you at all." She's asking me if this was really me. Now I have to say something coded to tell her that it wasn't.

"I wasn't feeling like myself," I agree. "You know how it is when you get your sights on one particular thing." Like harassment, or revenge. The funny thing is, I don't know whether there's actually a typo in there or not. I didn't look closely enough to notice. If not, she's really smart to have come up with that on the spot. I've always thought Janice was the enemy, but now when it matters, she's got my back. She hit the panic button strictly on my say so, before she even saw the guy's screen.

We toss around some innuendo. Janice is asking the guy whether he's ever done anything like this before. My heart is pounding too hard for me to pay close attention, especially since I'm straining to listen for sirens. Of course they won't come in that way, loud like a riot squad, but I'm listening for sirens anyway.

I'm listening so hard for the swish of the door that I don't hear it when it happens. I only know there's movement behind me because I see Janice's eyes follow it.

"Excuse me," she says to Vince. She hasn't handed his phone back to him. The doorway is, hopefully, now blocked by police. "Man soliciting sex from underage girl." She pushes her glasses up on her nose, talking as calmly as if she's reading it off a book catalog entry.

The guy turns and so do I. Two uniformed officers block the doorway. Now Vince's eyes are narrow; suspicious and cruel. "What is this? Is this a fucking sting?"

"Step away from the girl, sir," one of the officers says. His grip on my sleeve tightens, like he's considering doing something drastic, but then he drops his grasp with a tight scoff. *He's* mad at being set up? He could have stayed home. I'm the one who didn't get to consent to any of this.

He turns from me to the police. Both of them look like they work out way more than he does. He's panicked and worked up, but even still he seems to accept that there's nothing he can do. Fight isn't an option, and neither is flight.

The guy steps back, hands up. "I'd like my lawyer."

My skin burns where he grabbed me. "I'd like my parents," I say, "as long as we're asking for things."

My phone is evidence. The conversation he has on his is nowhere on mine, and I know it won't be found in the little virtual places where deleted things hide like skeletons in a digital closet. But that, too, is proof. This "Alison" Alliecat person wasn't me. Someone pretended to be me; probably had been pretending for a while. There are partial nude photos of someone that I don't know. They've been converted into black and white, probably to hide that the skin color doesn't match the yearbook photo they're using for my face.

An officer with *actual* kind eyes asks me a lot of questions, and gives me room to talk in my own words. The last name on his uniform is Burke. I want to remember that, because I want to write a letter to his department, thanking him for being gentle and kind. If this cop gets a letter, Janice is going to get an entire gift basket. I'm still stunned that she played along; that we were briefly, when it counted, a really good team.

The officer doesn't ask me who might have it out for me.

He doesn't ask me why this happened. He asks if I'd be more comfortable with a female officer, but I say no.

I make sure to tell him that Vince called me Alison. I'd never call myself Alison, because it's not my name. Yeah, I'm Allie, but it's short for Alicía. It's more evidence to exonerate me. Whoever did this, they had that big a grudge against me, but weren't paying enough attention to know my actual name.

A crowd is starting to gather, and I'm afraid to look for friendly faces in it. I don't know what to do if I find them.

As far as unfriendly faces, would whoever set this up be the type to stay far away so they can't get caught, or would they stay close enough to watch the scene unfold? It would depend on why they'd done it, I guess, and that's a thing I sure as hell can't answer. Because they hate me? Because they thought it would be funny? Because it's a day ending in Y and they were bored?

There are only two reasons not to ask me for insight into who set this up: either they don't care, or they already know.

Now I'm wondering where Paisley and Faith are. I'm also wondering what my dad was really doing that day when he asked me for my phone.

A hand on my shoulder makes me jump. It's Mom, with Brenna at her side. Dad is just past them, talking to one of the officers. I cling to my mother like a little kid. Vince, who's being led out of the library in cuffs, sees us, and it looks like it punches him in the gut. I look my age now, clinging to my mommies, and what he nearly did is sinking in. What *they* did is sinking in. Someone's just ruined his life and they don't care. He was just a pawn they were using to ruin mine.

"You were brave in there," Dad says on the way home. "I spoke to the county supervisor and she knows you had nothing to do with it. It won't be held against you. She and Janice both told me how hard you've worked to keep your job, despite unfair pressure from certain voices on the library board."

My cheeks burn. I'd worked equally hard to hide the fact that my job was in danger. So much for that.

"They have to take your computer, too," Dad says. "I'm sorry. It's just to clear your name. You'll get it back soon."

I should be grateful that it's so easy to prove I didn't instigate this mess, but my first thought is that I won't be able to tell Andrew or Keisha what's going on, or even explain why I'm out of touch.

"What does 'soon' look like?" I ask, as casually as I can.

"Hopefully by the end of the week. I've requested that they expedite on your equipment. Don't worry. It'll be fine. It's just standard procedure in cases like this. They have to be sure."

Makes sense. If I'd messaged that guy from home instead of from my phone, or whatever. So they'll see that I didn't, and move on to investigate whoever did.

In cases like this, he just said. "Do you see a lot of 'cases like this'?" I ask.

Dad gets quiet.

"Is there a suspect?" I ask, but Dad shakes his head. Not in a "no" way, but in a can't-tell-me way.

Andrew is waiting in our driveway, leaning against the back bumper of his Prius with his ankles crossed, like he's waiting for me to hurry up at the mall. It's so incongruously normal that I almost laugh. While our car idles, waiting for the garage door to open, I get out and vault into Andrew's arms.

"So… ?" Andrew prompts me, once we're safely ensconced in my room.

"So," I say. "Can you conference Ki in? I'd call her, but... no phone."

"Sure. Of course. I'm sorry I didn't think of it." He pulls out his phone and touches her portrait, then waits while it rings. "Hey, famous actress. I'm here with your girlfriend. It's been a fucking day. Do you have time to talk?"

"Yeah. Just let me..." I hear a metal door open and then bang closed. "Okay. Go."

I take a breath, then pause to make sure I have it right in my head. "So, if I'm reading all of this right, Paisley set some guy up to come screw me at work."

"Screw you?"

"Literally, screw me. In the stacks, or in the bathroom."

"Holy fuck," Keisha breathes. Andrew holds my hand tighter. I tell them about the dating site and the set-up, and the messages, and the digitally altered nudes that weren't me, and even how they'd covered the possibility that I wouldn't know who he was. "Oh—and don't be surprised if I don't answer your texts. It'll be up to a week before I get my phone back." I glance toward my desk, which looks sad and empty without my laptop.

Andrew rests the phone on my hip just as I go to hug him. The phone slides between us and he starts to retrieve it, and that's where his hand is when Dad knocks on the open door.

I cough, hold up the phone. "Hi, Dad. We're on speaker with Keisha."

"Hi, Keisha," Dad says. "Random fact." He comes in, pulls my desk chair out, and perches on the seat. He doesn't ask me to hang up so we can talk, but instead projects his voice to include her, over the phone. "A minor—someone who still counts as a child themselves—can still be charged with child pornography. Did you know, each photo—or explicit message—is one separate count of possession? Each message sent, or forwarded, or uploaded, is a count of distribution. Setting up a date between a minor and a non-minor is a count of solicitation."

He pauses.

I don't know where this is going. *What the hell did I have on my hard drive?*

"Another random fact: any website that requires a login, logs IP addresses of where those logins and attempts come from. IP tracking, unless people actively work to deceive it, is pretty accurate. So it's often possible to pinpoint where those people were when they connected."

My stomach peeks from somewhere around my ankles. I suspect it can let its butterflies out now. He's trying to tell me it's been traced and I'm in the clear.

"Cybercrimes are serious," Andrew says.

"True," Dad agrees. "So is the sex offender registry. Minors aren't exempt from that, either. It varies from state to state, but you're looking at a minimum of fifteen years before a person can get their name removed. I know gravestones that don't last as long as that." He shakes his head, sighs, and stands. "Thank you for being good kids. It makes this a lot easier. Okay. Dinner soon, so don't get too cozy."

We both stare at the door for a few long moments after he leaves.

Gravestones. A clever hint. So it was Paisley, at least in part. I hope her brother wasn't in on it. He seemed nice.

"If we'd sexted," Andrew says, "we'd have been guilty too."

"Not to mention, if he had to see anything like that from his own daughter, he'd want to bleach his eyes," Keisha adds.

I'm thinking about my search on pregnancy, but I just looked at the things that auto-completed and their previews.

I never actually clicked through. Hopefully that didn't show up anywhere.

"Did you know… does he work for… ?" Andrew doesn't finish the sentence, but I can fill in the blank.

"NSA? Cybercrimes? FBI? I don't know, but I always figured it was something like that. Now we know, huh?"

"Now we know."

"Thanks for not texting me your dick, Andrew."

He laughs. "Thanks, both of you, for not texting me nudes from the dressing room. Our indecent behavior is reserved for non-electronic communication only."

"An in-person bonus." I manage a grin, then add, for Keisha, "Which you'll be back here collecting before you know it."

"I love you guys," she says. "I have to get back, but thank you for including me. Talk soon?"

"Talk soon," I agree. "One… two…" and Andrew ends the call.

I meet his pale eyes for a long, reassuring moment. We barely have time to kiss before my parents call us down to dinner.

CHAPTER 16

'M still reeling, and I can't pretend I'm not. Andrew's hand in mine steadies me, keeps me tethered to the moment. Keeps me feeling safe.

Brenna is still dressed from work and so is Mom. Dad has changed into jeans, with a faded gray t-shirt that says "offline mode." I put a hand to my pocket where my phone should be. His irony isn't lost on me.

Dad sees me looking and plucks at his shirt. "In solidarity," he says. I hug him.

Mom wraps me, then Andrew, in tight hugs. Brenna hugs us too.

"You were so brave," Mom says. I feel my cheeks flush. I mean, I was brave, yes, but I'm not sure how to respond.

We settle in around the table. "It's a comfort food day," Brenna says, bringing over a plate of halved grilled cheese sandwiches she's kept warm in the oven. They're buttery and melty and crisp. I wasn't hungry, but when the smell reaches me I'm reminded how food is a good, good thing. There's tomato soup, too, which she serves in mugs.

"It all happened so fast," I say. "And it made no *sense*."

"Tell me?" Brenna says.

I glance toward Dad, and Andrew takes my hand under the table.

"This girl Paisley who volunteers at the library—it was her grandparents' tombstone that I hit. And ever since, she's been all over me. It's like she's trying to get me fired, even though I obviously need the job in order to pay back *her* family. And then she started getting her friends into it, including Loudon across the street."

"Which was also," Dad says, "when there was a hacking attempt on our home wifi network."

"How did you know?" Andrew asks, at the same time I ask, "Is that why you wanted my phone?"

Dad gives Andrew a pointed look without answering. Then he turns that same look on me. "Trade secrets," he answers, to both of us. "What matters is that the attempt failed, and once I was aware of it, I could take... actions."

"Did you know what they were doing?" I ask.

"No." Dad shakes his head. "I didn't know who it was, or what they were trying to do. Then I learned that there had been attempts to access certain blocked sites from the library computers."

"The library has cameras," I tell him.

"Yes. And computer timestamps plus camera timestamps..."

"Equals who I think it equals?" I ask.

He pauses, but then he nods. He picks a word carefully: "Allegedly." He passes the plate to me, but I shake my head. I've eaten a half of a sandwich and my stomach is too jumpy for me to attempt more.

"So, what happens to the... allegedly guilty party?" Andrew asks.

"She's taken into custody, though her parents have probably already posted bail. So she's probably at home and in a lot of trouble, and it's unlikely you'll see her in the library again."

"No tears over that. What about the guy she duped?"

Dad's face drops. It's so easy to be taken in by people who aren't what they seem. I feel bad for the guy, but only a little. The fact that he was willing to go through with it keeps me from being too sympathetic.

"It'll depend on his prior behavior. His electronic footprint will show what he thought he was getting into."

"As in, whether he knew 'Alison' was a minor?" Andrew asks.

"Right. Exactly that."

As for the people who set him up, they absolutely knew. They probably thought it was a prank. I'm sure they did. I can't imagine they'd have done it if they realized it was such a serious crime.

I'm back at work the next day. My knees are trembling and I startle at every sound and voice, but showing up is nine-tenths of... something, right?

What's important is that anyone who cares can see that I'm in the library today and that they didn't beat me. Janice says that if anyone asks I can tell them that I can't talk about it because I'm working, but they can ask her for details. She'll confirm that no, I'm not in trouble.

No one asks. A few people whisper, but no one asks.

The computers are gone from the media room, but people are sitting at the empty desks reading and stuff, as if that's what those tables have always been for. Paisley doesn't show up, even though she was on the schedule. Here too, no one says anything. And without Paisley, there's no Faith.

I knew Paisley was behind it, but there's a difference between knowing internally and actually seeing knowledge confirmed. Why else wouldn't she be here, when she should be gloating and smirking at having freaked me out so much, and at ruining some poor random guy's life. Ruining lives is probably what she does as a hobby. I wonder if there are any colleges that accept life-ruining as an extracurricular, because "sex offender" isn't going to look great on her transcript.

Her mother is off the library board. Not that they come out and say it, but a notice tacked up on the bulletin board says that there'll be a special election next month for an open seat.

Inventory done, I go up front to check in some books. Business as usual. Business as usual. I repeat it to myself in my head.

Janice, at some point, comes up beside me. She hands, I scan. "Good to see you, Diaz," she says. Quietly, of course, so that she won't have to shush herself. I imagine what that would look like and it makes me smile. "There's our girl," she says, even though she doesn't know what I'm smiling about. But it's not awkward. It's extra touching, if anything, that she doesn't care why I'm happy, just that I am.

And, you know, maybe I am. Things are quiet. I feel almost safe.

I get my phone and computer back on Friday. Dad brings them home from work with him. I can imagine him asking the techs to please rush them because he doesn't know how much longer he can survive with an internet-deprived teenager in the house.

"You're not under suspicion, so there's no reason to hold onto them," he says, bursting that bubble. "They imaged your hard drives, so they've got a copy to look at if they need anything, but you've been cleared."

"Because my IP address doesn't match where the messages were sent from?" I ask. He doesn't say anything, but he ruffles my hair in that I'm-proud-of-you way that means yes.

"I think Paisley and Faith were filming it, till it went bad," I tell him. "I hope someone recovers that video and they incriminate themselves on it."

"I think the odds of that are very high. Also, you got a letter."

Dad gives me an envelope textured like linen. The paper is beige, but too thick to see the contents through it. It's been slit neatly across the top with a letter opener, above the embossed address of a law firm, so I know he knows what it says, but I dutifully pull the crisp page out for myself.

And I laugh. It's a manic laugh, kind of hysterical, and Dad just smirks faintly until I've caught my breath.

Paisley has a lawyer, of course. This letter, via her lawyer, is her official apology for any mental and emotional hardship her actions may have caused. She was jealous because her brother liked me, and she didn't see why I had to date the whole world, and she thought my punishment after the accident was too light.

That's a lot to admit, and a lot to take in.

It goes on to say that her family is willing to write off our debt to them—the cost of replacing the tombstone—as a good-will gesture that they hope we'll return with gentle testimony and forgiveness when this eventually goes to court. After all, kids will be kids, and she had no idea how serious a turn her antics would take.

I fold the letter, slide it gently into the envelope, and hand it back to Dad.

"I made a mistake and I owned it," I say. "She can do the same. She doesn't get to buy her way out."

Dad puts his arm around me and I curl in against him. "I think that's a good call. That's how we'll respond."

Loudon's videos have been taken down. It's really hard to get a video removed from the internet, but her whole account is gone. Faith is facing probation and community service, at the least. No one is coming out and saying Paisley was the ringleader, which makes it hard to find out what she thought messing with me was going to accomplish, but it looks like there's been a wide-spread realization that making someone miserable just because you feel like it can lead to real world consequences.

And, I've realized, so can love.

Growing up in the little bubble of polyamorous harmony that my parents have made, it looks easy. It looks accepted. So maybe I got a little complacent and forgot that it's not the norm. It's definitely not the norm in high school.

Hearts are jerks, though. They don't listen to anyone or anything. Not to sense, not to reason, and definitely not to us. Sometimes they fall for someone you wish they wouldn't. Sometimes they fall for someone great and they buoy you, and it's still a lot of work to make a go of things. Sometimes they fall for more than one person at a time.

Some people dismiss or ignore it when that happens. I choose not to. I can't help who—or how many people—I love. It wouldn't be love if I could just turn it off when it wasn't convenient. If there was a way to do that, people would have found it by now. Anyway, I'm not sure I'd want to. The turbulence pushes at where you're weak and challenges you to strengthen yourself, I think.

With Keisha moving, we knew communication was going to be our weak spot, we just didn't know how that would manifest. Maybe next time I'll make a different mistake, or she will, but we'll make it through this stupid year and still be together when she comes back. Even if we don't end up at the same college.

I'm determined talk with her about that, and I'm not frightened anymore that she'll be upset. She's found her passions and I've found mine, and we can both still have room to be passionate for each other, too. I think it's okay if we're not always on exactly the same trajectory, as long as we support each other's successes and feel safe communicating when things are low.

No... I don't just think. I'm sure of it.

AUTHOR'S NOTE

How many polyamorous people are there?
We don't know. It's not a question on the census, and it's not a thing people readily disclose. Polyamory is still illegal in 21 U.S. states under current adultery laws, and in 2012 about 40% polyamorous people reported experiencing some sort of discrimination in the past 10 years (28.5% more than the general U.S. population).[1]

In 2012, Loving More, with the endorsement of the National Coalition of Sexual Freedom, conducted an internet-based survey of participants who self-identified as polyamorous. This was the largest such survey to date, attracting over 4000 participants.

According to a 2016 U.S. study[2], 1 in 5 Americans reported having been in a non-monogamous relationship. Also in 2016, a Canadian study by the Canadian Research Institute for Law and the Family (CRILF) found 547 voluntary respondents.[3]

As for children in polyamorous families, the Canadian study found that 23% of respondents said that at least one child under the age of 19 lived full-time in their household. A 2018 study published in the Journal of Sex Research surveyed nearly 2500 polyamorous participants and found that approximately 30% of them had children in their households (showing no statistical difference from monogamous individuals surveyed)[4].

Courts in the United States and Canada (in 2017 and 2018, respectively) have ruled in favor of three adults being treated as legal parents of a minor, and in California a statute was passed in 2013 acknowledging that a child may have more than two parents.

With television shows like *Big Love*, *Married and Dating*, and smaller-network or independent shows like *You Me Her* and *Unicornland* spotlighting the vicarious sexual aspect of polyamory with their popularity, and self-help books providing thought experiments in how polyamory might ideally work if a reader and their family unit wanted to try it for themselves, there is no denying its popularity as an entertainment and a social movement.

But what about the children?

Dr. Elisabeth Sheff performed a 20-year study of children growing up in polyamorous households. She discovered that very young children make no distinction between their family structure and the family structures of others. Teens, however, are well aware that their families are different. "In addition to navigating the complexities of coming from an unconventional family, these teens must decide what it means for their own budding sexuality." [2]

It's my hope that *Hearts Are Jerks* will help people with polyamorous families or polyamorous leanings to find themselves in a society that constantly tries to tell us there is only one way to live our lives.

"When readers are able to find themselves in a text, they are therefore validated; their experiences are not so unique or strange as to never be spoken or experienced by others" says Taylor Cavalovitch of Duquesne University.[5] Representation in fiction is important, and unfortunately many people on the fringe don't have a good sampling of representational role models to choose from. Scholarly and first-person accounts confirm the formative influence of fictional role models on children and teens. [5] [6] [7][8]

About Hearts Are Jerks

Because each relationship and situation is as unique as the people who comprise it, there are no hard-and-fast rules for success. Instead, this book is a work of fiction which offers some situations, both typical and unusual, and some outcomes.

The core of this novel is a supportive family with a certain amount of wealth and privilege. I don't mean to suggest it as the typical family. Rather, it's an ideal condition. Supportive parents and stable households may induce wistful feelings in some readers, but showing a functional home is important:

- It shows in the simple and idealized forms how conflicts might resolve.
- It shows relationships of different kinds and at different stages.
- It removes the idea that trauma creates alternate sexualities and relationship models. No traumatic childhoods or unmet needs turned anyone here queer or polyamorous.
- Orientation doesn't need a reason, and certainly doesn't need an excuse. These are mostly-neurotypical, well-adjusted characters, and they don't always know the answers.

So the rest of us surely can't be expected to.

But maybe sitting in and watching them for a while might help.

Gabrielle Harbowy
Southern California, December, 2019

REFERENCES

[1] https://www.lovingmorenonprofit.org/polyamory-articles/2012-lovingmore-polyamory-survey/

[2] https://www.psychologytoday.com/us/blog/the-polyamorists-next-door/201704/children-in-polyamorous-families-part-1

[3] https://ablawg.ca/2016/08/24/polyamorous-canada-early-results-from-crilf

[4] https://www.researchgate.net/profile/Rhonda_Balzarini/publication/325834758_Demographic_comparison_of_American_individuals_in_polyamorous_and_monogamous_relationships/links/5b2930bea6fdcc72dbedeb6a/Demographic-comparison-of-American-individuals-in-polyamorous-and-monogamous-relationships.pdf?origin=publication_detail

[5] https://dsc.duq.edu/cgi/viewcontent.cgi?article=1003&context=urss

[6] https://www.buzzfeed.com/farrahpenn/ya-authors-on-diverse-representation-in-publishi

[7] https://files.eric.ed.gov/fulltext/EJ787934.pdf

[8] https://www.psychologytoday.com/us/blog/thinking-about-kids/201205/i-could-do-why-role-models-matter

LEGAL CASES:

https://www.cbc.ca/news/canada/newfoundland-labrador/polyamourous-relationship-three-parents-1.4706560

https://verdict.justia.com/2013/10/15/california-allows-children-two-legal-parents

https://abovethelaw.com/2017/03/court-grants-custody-to-three-parents-we-may-not-need-duncles-much-longer/

ACKNOWLEDGMENTS

GREAT love and thanks to Matt and Steve, for much healthy modeling and support, and to Amy, Christa, Gavin, and Jamie, for providing the same while parenting. Rainforest Writers Retreat gets credit for giving me and David a 15-hour drive in which to work out the plot, and the perfect space and ambiance to dig into my characters' lives once I got there.

Thanks to Marie and Kerri for loaning me their cat Pamplo, known here as Ozone. Editor Jamie Wyman saved me from my continuity errors, as always. Gwen Gades designed a perfect cover. Leah gave me valuable help and insight into the publication process, and Garnet Griffin designed the beautiful logo for Heart Bow Books.

ABOUT THE AUTHOR

GABRIELLE HARBOWY is an award-nominated editor, author, and anthologist. She is the author of the novels *Of the Essence* and *Pathfinder Tales: Gears of Faith*, and numerous short stories. She has edited five anthologies, including the acclaimed *When the Hero Comes Home* series with Ed Greenwood, and *The Complete Guide to Writing For Young Adults, Vol 1*. She has a degree in Psychology from Rutgers University, and has been living an ethically polyamorous life since her early 20s. For more information, visit her online at gabrielleharbowy.com.

ALSO BY
GABRIELLE HARBOWY

Made in the USA
Columbia, SC
06 March 2020